"Do you want to kiss me, m'sieu?"

Patch's eyes were a glossy black as she looked up at Cooper. Sexual currents were surging between them, making her reel. "Do you want to?" she repeated urgently.

"I believe I do," Cooper said hoarsely. Their mouths came together, and a moan of pleasure broke from deep within his chest. "I want more than a kiss," he went on, pressing his thighs to hers.

There was no doubt of his meaning, Patch realized; he was as aroused as she. And a fierce and secret fire began to burn at her very core....

THE AUTHOR

Jackie Weger writes some of the most unique love stories published and has countless adventures in the process. While researching *Beneath a Saffron Sky* she went out in the Atchefalaya Basin with Cajun trappers—and experienced the cold snap described in the story.

With her husband, Jackie lives in Fort Bend County, Texas. But her familiarity with many other areas and her own natural curiosity are a great combination in finding unusual settings—and plots— for her books.

Books by Jackie Weger

HARLEQUIN TEMPTATION

HARLEQUIN AMERICAN ROMANCE

These books may be available at your local bookseller.

Don't miss any of our special offers. Write to us at the following address for information on our newest releases.

Harlequin Reader Service
P.O. Box 52040, Phoenix, AZ 85072-2040
Canadian address: P.O. Box 2800, Postal Station A,
5170 Yonge St., Willowdale, Ont. M2N 6J3

Beneath a Saffron Sky

JACKIE WEGER

Harlequin Books

TORONTO • NEW YORK • LONDON
AMSTERDAM • PARIS • SYDNEY • HAMBURG·
STOCKHOLM • ATHENS • TOKYO • MILAN

For Courtney and Melissa

————◆————

Thanks to
Richard and Earline Domangue
Freddie and Delores Cox
Alles and Tina Billiot

————◆————

Published April 1985

ISBN 0-373-25153-X

1

A SMALL WINTER-WIND rustled drooping willows that grew along the bayou. Patch's eyes swept the swamp, seeing nothing dangerous, nothing out of place, nothing that she hadn't seen every single day of her life. Evergreen pine soared toward a dusk-ridden sky. Fat cypress stumps squatted on their gnarled roots, keeping company with a shadowy underbrush of which she knew every inch, and every mile. Beneath the boat the tide flowed on its ceaseless march with the moon, covering sandbars and bog, and these she knew, too, though they shifted, grew and ebbed with the seasons. Still she felt uneasy and restless, filled with a strange qualm.

Looking back over her shoulder, she surveyed the lacy wake of the boat, the scattered fog drifts that were chasing her home. She sighed heavily, annoyed with the prickling at the back of her neck. She was just in a scratchy mood, most prob'ly. It had started that morning at first light and had clung like tentacles all day, causing her to constantly check the sky, peer into black water and watch the swamp like a wary fox with a litter of newborn kits who knows a hawk is soaring on an updraft, seeking out prey.

She had felt time and again that something—anything!—was going to happen, yet the old motor had throbbed unfailingly, her nets had not been tampered with and the price of fish had not dropped alarmingly. Now the mood still tugged at her, stron-

ger. Must be trapping anxiety, now that she thought
about it. There were a hundred ten things to do, to
not forget, before the season opened. A partner
would go a long way in keeping things straight, she
thought wistfully, but she didn't have one and
wasn't likely to. She couldn't afford a partner, not
even on shares. She shrugged impatiently, shifting
her hand on the throttle to shut off the motor, and
with a light touch on the tiller guided the thirty-foot
workhorse of a boat against an aging pier. On the
first bump she moved swiftly from the stern thwart
to make it fast to a barnacle-encrusted piling.

Before climbing from the old high-sided boat,
Patch stood and gazed a moment at the house on the
levee, in which she'd been born. From uncurtained
parlor windows golden light escaped, beckoning
and warm. A shadow of anguish blazed in her troubled dark eyes. The friendly light was deceiving...
not that *maman* had said anything mean outright,
but she'd been acting resentful a fearful lot lately.

Patch tried for an instant to look into the sky to
find the stars and so find the path of her prayers, but
the gray rolling mists had risen above the scrub oak
and towering pines, hiding the stars from view. No
matter; she knew they were there. Her prayers were
always getting snagged on one star or the other—
trapped, most prob'ly, as she trapped nutria, mink
and muskrat—so they never reached that special
place in heaven where the wishes and hopes of the
living were gathered.

If God liked her, Patch thought, if He heard her
prayers, He would send her a man, one who had the
patience to wait out the pledge she had made to her
sister Rosalina. Not a man like Arlis Lafargue, who
had abandoned her to take up with Una LaBlanc—
cow-eyed Una of the big breasts, who was already
thick with child. *Not* like Arlis Lafargue, Patch

sniffed, aiming the thought heavenward just in case it happened to find unencumbered portage.

In the gossamer privacy of the mists, Patch's hand crept beneath her coat to touch her breasts. They might swell, stand erect, shouting at a man's touch, but it was a very small shout, from very small breasts. She was diminutive, true. But having been toughened by hard work, she did not think of herself as delicate; fishing, trapping and hunting in all manner of weather had given her a strength beyond her small stature. Men ought not ask for more, she thought, but they did. Still, she could do anything her papa had done, and there were those who said better, because she hadn't the thirst that papa had had. There was no sense bewailing her fate.

She had enough flesh on her bones to be called woman and a woman's pride in the way she carried herself, so that whether she was observed poling a pirogue or gliding across marsh bog, dressed in cords or hip-high boots, observers felt drawn to watch until she was out of view. There was something indefinable and provocative about her, as though she were one with the wild desolate expanse of the swamp. But her clear and bottomless black eyes beneath a wide forehead were what made one suspect a brooding vulnerability camouflaged in strength and skill. She had a lovely mouth, quick to smile, and that endeared her to her friends, but of late she hadn't smiled often.

Feeling the chill of the night, Patch removed her hip-high rubber boots, tossing them atop fishnets in the bottom of the boat, hefted her rifle and scrambled onto the sagging pier. After checking to make certain the boat was secure against tide or mishap, she trudged up the steeply inclined walk to emerge into a windswept dogtrot. The open-ended porch with its cambered roof separated the kitchen and

parlor from sleeping rooms. It was always breezy—
green and cool in summer, frigid in winter.

Despite the promise of warmth inside, Patch leaned
her head against the great thick door, suddenly feeling weak and lifeless. Her hand rose to pat a pocket
that held the money she'd received for the day's catch.
The fine crinkle gave her reassurance. *Maman* would
be pleased. Slowly, silently, gathering strength from
the sharp icy air, she lifted the heavy iron latch and
entered the cheerful warmth and good cooking smells
that filled the steam-filled kitchen.

A low murmur of conversation came to a halt the
instant she crossed the threshold. Her dark eyes
widened, flicking toward Grand-mère Duval, who
was tottering between table and stove. The old
woman was wearing a starched, embroidered apron
over her long brown dress, the one she always wore
when preparing dinner for Grand-père Duval's
ghost. There was *maman*, sitting at her usual place,
her ebony hair done up in a tidy knot atop her head,
her shriveled leg with its heavy shoe tucked carefully behind the other. And finally...Patch's gaze
came to rest on the man who was rising from papa's
chair. The greeting to her mother and her grandmother died on her lips.

She stared at the man, the most elegant man she'd
ever seen, while her heart went fluttering like a
newly hatched butterfly drying its wings. The fluttering chased all breath from her lungs so that she
was obliged to part her lips to let in air.

God had never answered any of her prayers. Not
one! Not when she was fifteen and had prayed for
good trapping so they'd have enough money to go
down to Mardi Gras in New Orleans. Not two years
ago when she prayed that Arlis would take her up to
Red's Levee Bar for her twenty-first birthday. He
hadn't answered when she'd prayed desperately

that papa be found alive, and above all, He had not healed Rosalina. Yet here was a man.... She closed the door soundlessly, as she had been taught to do as a child, without a word or a cry to betray her astonishment.

The man was taller than she, not much, though being built of thick muscle and lean sinew, he had more substance. Clean limbed, she thought, when she could manage to think at all. He was wearing a dark tweed suit fitted to his broad shoulders, and a red tie lay casually undone below the open collar of a snowy lawn shirt. He had an unruly thatch of blond hair and the lively eyes of a cynic, stern and keen. His most singular feature was his jaw: square, knobby and confident. His face was grooved either side of a straight nose set above a well-cut mouth. The edges of his mouth lifted now with a slight expectant smile. His blue eyes were looking at her with a question, calculating, measuring her, so that Patch knew *maman* had not mentioned her existence. The stranger had an aura about him, as though he knew exactly what he wanted and was quite sure of getting it. She recognized in him that quality found in wary hunters who are familiar with hazard; men who protect their flanks even as they spy out their forward step. Lor! But she needed a man like that.

She opened her mouth to speak but bit down on her tongue just in time. God had a way of snatching what she most wanted to His bosom just as she was reaching for it. Desperately Patch tried to recall at least one of the many things she had planned to talk about with her mother, nice things that would take *maman*'s mind from papa's dying, and from Rosalina, hospitalized in Baton Rouge. But she couldn't remember a single one.

"Patch," Natalie Chauvin commanded, sharp edged, "don't stand there like a startled deer. You have manners, no? Come greet our new boarder, Cooper Vachec." The expression on her face warned her daughter not to dispute her.

"Boarder?" Patch repeated, stunned. Surprise made her speak in lilting Cajun French, and her dark eyes flashed.

"Speak English," her mother ordered.

"I hope I won't be intruding," Cooper Vachec was saying pleasantly. His voice, deep, soft and carrying, rang over Patch like the distant beat of galloping hoofs. She watched in renewed wonder as he came fluidly toward her, holding out his hand, the grooves alongside his nose growing deeper, thinner, with his smile. Oh, lor! He had a million white teeth.

The weary prickling that had plagued her slipped like satin from her shoulders. There had never been a boarder in the Chauvin house. Company, yes. A boarder—never. She shifted the rifle from one hand to the other, yanked off her knit cap, letting her short brown curls burst free, and tucked it under her arm as she advanced toward him. Somehow she managed to unstick her tongue from the roof of her mouth. "If *maman* says not, you won't, *m'sieu.*"

She touched his hand lightly, but her fingertips caught fire and she jerked them back.

Natalie's face shouted disapproval. For the first time in many months, Patch ignored her mother. She kept her eyes fastened on Cooper Vachec, gazing at him so hard he thought his fly might be open.

He moved hurriedly back to his chair, annoyed that the girl was staring at him as if he was the answer to a prayer. Unobtrusively, when he replaced his napkin in his lap, he checked his zipper. Closed. He emitted a faint sigh.

Grand-mère Duval brushed past Patch, placing a platter of fried oysters on the table before Cooper. "Dreaming doesn't cost anything," she announced, as though it were some morsel in addition to the oysters. "It's like hope. You kep on and on...." She tilted her head on her once-regal neck and smiled.

Patch caught the surprised expression on Cooper Vachec's face at her grandmother's words. She started to protest, but it was no use because *grand-mère* was moving her lips soundlessly and that meant she had left their world for a little while.

"Start dinner without me, *maman*," Patch said, and without waiting for a reply, moved toward the bathroom.

"We have company," called Natalie sternly, so that Patch understood she was to have no time to herself, no time to sort the turmoil beginning now to spin questions in her mind.

She threw off her heavy jacket, her flannel shirt, her insulated undershirt, grabbing a well-worn cotton blouse off a hook and tucking it into snug-fitting pants that hugged the curve of her hips and the shape of her legs. She brushed her balky brown curls, cut short in concession to conditions in the swamp, until they gleamed and formed a dark helmet about her face, which when it wasn't tanned from sun or red from winter winds, was lustrous and creamy. Then she scrubbed the smell of fish from her hands.

Her hands, callused as the man's were not—that had registered in their brief clasp. Somehow it stung her femininity. She took an extra few seconds to massage them with perfumed lotion, and knowing that she would subject herself to more barbs from Natalie if she took a minute longer, she emerged quietly from the bathroom and slipped into her chair at the table.

Her hunger had disappeared, replaced by an odd inner excitement that rose and fell with every breath, inciting such a spreading warmth within her that she feared she might melt and slide off her chair into a puddle under the table.

She pretended indifference, but watched Cooper fixedly, listening to every scrap of conversation between him and her mother, trying to delve into his character, searching for the things she wanted most in a man. She sensed in him an anger but couldn't define the source. Patch suspected it went deeper than the slight shift of annoyance she could read in his eyes, though he smiled deceptively at Natalie. She willed him to turn his gaze to her, and when he didn't she cast her eyes down, stirring food on her plate. Some of her joy slid off center.

He was not a tourist; he didn't have that gushing enthusiasm. Her curiosity about him rose, especially the reason for his requiring lodging.

Grand-mère made a little fuss as she took her place at the table. God and His multitude of saints, the devil and his nefarious workers and Grand-père Duval's ghostly spirit had always been a part of Patch's existence. In the swamp, like everywhere else, the seasons changed from summer to fall, from life to death. Disease, predation, old age all took their toll. The old buck given to dreaming of his rutting youth cobbled his antlers fast in the crook of a tree, his horns becoming fodder for cotton rats who in turn fed the hawk. It was all the same to Grand-mère Duval, whose fodder was her past. When, like now, she was having one of her spells—setting a place at the table for *grand-père*, believing that he was coming home from war—it was easier to indulge her than argue. But there were two extra settings at the table. Patch touched *grand-mère*'s gnarled old hand. "Do we have more than one guest?" she asked in Cajun.

The old woman shook her off. "I see another soul soaring on the wings of the great white bird."

"You mean *grand-père* has asked another . . . soul to supper?"

"Stop talking silly, both of you," Natalie put in, smiling an apology to Cooper, though Patch knew he could not have understood the exchange.

Grand-mère Duval turned her beady dark eyes on her daughter. "Villany is not silly. Duval has company."

Natalie blanched and, for the space of a breath, Patch thought her mother would not contain her anger. But they had a guest at table, and she did. Natalie was not as tolerant of *grand-mère*'s old-woman ways and loose mind as was Patch.

"I have to tend to some things, *maman*," she said, excusing herself. Cooper looked fully at her then, but it was too late for her to change her mind and stay at the table.

"We have a guest to entertain," reminded Natalie, halting her escape. "Build up the fire in the parlor. We'll take our coffee there."

Louisiana had no natural stone formations, and the granite rocks that made up the chimney were said to have once been ballast in ships belonging to the Lafitte brothers. Patch did not discount this legend because papa's family had been among the French laborers from the old world who had helped raise New Orleans out of the mud. Chauvins had hunted and trapped and lived along the silt-fed waterways and bayous for hundreds of years.

By the time the fire of pine knots was blazing to her liking, Cooper strolled into the parlor—alone. Patch straightened, facing him, forcing him to acknowledge her presence as he had not at the dining table.

"What brings you to the Atchafalaya Basin, *m'sieu*?" she asked, discovering that her breath was hung up somewhere between her heart and her throat.

"I've contracted to do a field study for the Environmental Protection Agency—"

Her entire body went rigid. "You're government?" Her lilting tone was strangled. She closed her eyes, her lashes lying entrancingly along her cheeks while the wonderful vision she'd been entertaining shriveled like a rose beneath a desert sun. Nothing good for the swamp had ever come out of government messing with their lives. She raised her lashes, revealing eyes smoldering like molton lava. "Does *maman* know?"

"Who?"

"*Maman*—my mother."

His expression mocked her. "Yes."

"Traitors, all!" She spoke the words harshly, turning away from him to stare into the fire. Cooper Vachec was now beneath notice.

The parlor was a quaint, impeccably neat room having a kind of old grandeur in the stiff, sugar-starched antimacassars on the backs of chairs and in the leaded lamps shedding light on tables. A highboy, richly carved and burnished with oil, held court against one wall, while votive candles flickered in tiny red cups on a wooden shelf beneath a molded brass crucifix. The smell of the burning wicks was evocative, blending as it did with burning pine knots. The flames of both cast moving, shadowy phantoms on the low-beamed ceiling.

Wire taut, her back to him and watching the fire shifting in the grate, Patch knew the man was surveying her. She sensed his rancor, but she was finished with him—guest or not.

"Mind if I smoke?" His voice ricocheted off her back. She turned to look at him, and Cooper couldn't keep from noticing how very wide, how very dark her eyes were, and how laced with fury.

"Suit yourself, *m'sieu*." She returned to the mesmerizing flames.

Resolutely Cooper lit up. He was in an unreasoning mood born of an overwhelming combination of things—little worrisome, nettlesome, nerve-pricking things that taken alone would have had no effect on him. He had tried to put off this assignment in the middle of winter and had failed. He'd had two flats on the drive down from Washington—the same damn tire. The New Orleans office had given him the name of a guide who had been dead for a year. Now he stood in the dead man's house being railed at by a swamp sprite so tiny he could have folded her up and put her in his back pocket. He had sensed the hostility between mother and daughter, and that contributed to his annoyance. To top it off, he was warring with a peculiar sensation—wanting this girl to like him. She was appealing, though he hadn't been able to put an exact name to her appeal. It aroused his ire that she found him wanting.

At the dinner table, though rankled, he had smiled at the mother and had listened with half an ear to the astonishing ramblings of the grandmother. But each time the girl had lifted her cup, picked up her fork or offered some gentle command to the old woman he had known it. He had noted her face, lightly tanned; had noted the slight opening of her shirt that gave a hint, no more, of creamy skin and intriguing hollows. Under the cotton fabric her small rounded breasts rose and fell, causing a stirring in his loins that he studiously ignored. There was going to be trouble before this job was over, he knew. He could feel it in his bones. He blew smoke into the air and watched it trail ceilingward.

Natalie came into the parlor bearing coffee service

on a wooden, much-used tray. She took short minc-
ing steps to lessen the drag on her crippled leg.

Patch refused coffee. "I had my fill earlier." She
knew she sounded brusque, but she was twisted into
knots and pressing for escape.

"Have one cup with us, Patch," Natalie said. "To
be friendly, yes?"

She wanted to decline again, but her mother
knew she would show no disrespect in front of
their guest—despite his government affiliation. "One,
then," she answered, giving Cooper a cool unwaver-
ing look and taking her cup to a small stool nearer the
fire. Her ill grace was smoothly deflected.

"Patch is sometimes tired and testy at this time of
evening," remarked Natalie.

"I thought it was me she objected to," Cooper said.
He was spoiling for a fight—or a good laugh to lessen
the tension. It had been stupid to hunt up the guide
this late at night. He should have bunked down in a
motel, instead of accepting Natalie's hospitality.

"I do object to you," Patch said silkily, aiming a
look at him that was alive with mysterious under-
currents. "All you people do is come in here and
make rules. Licenses for this and that... boats, fishing, trapping, hunting—"

Cooper stiffened. "That's State, not—"

Patch was fired up now, angry at God, at Cooper,
at Natalie, and especially at herself, for hoping when
she knew it was no use. Her dark eyes ignited with
battle. "I suppose the fact that hundreds of people
were moved out of the swamp so the government
could flood us out if they wanted to is 'State'? Our
family is one of the lucky ones. A far-thinking an-
cestor built upon high ground that later was connected to the levee. But many of our friends have
been moved out, leaving behind them the only way
of life they know."

Her attack on him was unjustified, filled with anger. Yet there as a trace of sadness in her strained tone—a suggestion that she had suffered sorrow in the past and expected more in the future. His reply was softer than he'd meant. "That was the Corps of Engineers."

"Government is government." Patch slipped off the stool and backed up to the fire, squaring her softly rounded shoulders. Talking was easier when one stood on one's feet.

"Patch, apologize to Cooper. You're being unfriendly. That's not the Cajun way." Natalie flashed a warning to her daughter before turning a bright look on Cooper. "More coffee, yes?"

Go on, unleash your charm, maman, Patch thought, *it won't do any good. Nothing does with these government types. They're cold.*

"Thank you," Cooper replied, blandly examining the burning tip of his cigarette. No apology came from the girl, and he could feel her vibrating with vexation. He lifted his eyes to her slowly, giving her his best smile. There were women who said he had an adorable smile. "I agree with you that there's too much government bureaucracy, but your own legislators and congressmen make the laws. The Environmental Protection Agency only follows them. All *I* do is gather information—scientists and statisticians analyze it."

"To what purpose?" Patch said, sniffing, charmed only a little by his grin. "To tell us what we already know? Our swamplands are shrinking? We don't need you for that, and we don't need anyone to tell us how to preserve it. We *know*—keep people like you out."

"Daughter, daughter, you're being rude, no? And to a guest under our own roof."

When Natalie called her "daughter," Patch knew

she had gone too far. She drew a deep acquiescing
breath. She still felt inflamed but made an effort to
control her temper, and the disappointment that
lingered at the edge of her dreams...her prayers.
Avoiding her mother's eyes, she took the tray,
placed it on a side table and refilled their cups. She
handed Cooper his with a steady hand, adopting a
pleasant demeanor. "Where do you work, mostly?"

"Washington, D.C."

"A deskman."

Cooper took a sip of the sweet, cream-tinted brew,
then with subtle purposeful indifference lowered
the cup from his mouth. "Perhaps I should find
other quarters."

Patch told herself she had no use for Cooper
Vachec, but now her breath caught so low in her
chest, she thought for an instant that she'd have to
be pounded on the back to get it up again.

"Oh, no, *m'sieu*," Natalie cried shooting a flus-
tered look at Patch. "We Cajuns just like to argue.
It's in our blood, no? Patch was just having fun with
you. Isn't that so, daughter?"

Patch stirred more sugar into her coffee. "Prob'ly.
We're hotheaded sometimes." She wasn't about to
give in too easily. A man like him would take it to be
a weakness. What she'd like to give in to most was
the urge to exit, leaving the man to her mother's
charm, which was flowing as thick as swamp mud.
If only papa was here, or Rosalina.... She bent her
head and buried the thoughts in a far recess of her
brain. She lived and worked in a world of stark realities, not a wishing well.

"How well do you know the swamp?"

Patch snapped alert, slanting a look at Cooper.
"Very well, *m'sieu*." A tilt of her delicate chin be-
spoke an unbearable pride. He was aware again of
that hint of appeal she held for him, and he came

closer to identifying it. "I've lived here all my life. I fish and trap and hunt. I went with my papa until he died, now I go about it alone. I never get lost."

He was thinking he'd had enough, that he shouldn't ask, but he knew he was going to. It was all her fault, he thought darkly. Egging him on, challenging him like she had.... "I still need a guide. I'm not familiar—"

"Not me, *m'sieu*," Patch said, appalled, catching his drift. If she had any truck with a government man, her friends and neighbors would begin casting suspicious glances. No trapper wanted officials messing about his lease. "I don't have time. Trapping season begins in a few days. There's camp to be set up, supplies to haul, traps to clean and set out. Our lease has to be worked this year or we'll see it go to someone else."

Cooper frowned. He was used to getting his way with women, and here was one turning him down. He didn't like being rejected. Leaning forward, he said, "I'd appreciate it if you'd reconsider. This isn't the kind of work that one hurries. I need to take samples, to check the soil banks dredged from canals for pollutants, to observe winter water swells and the rise in silt—nothing very earth shattering. Perhaps I could even be of some help to you," he argued. "I don't want to be an imposition, and I'd pay you well."

"With government money, no doubt."

His face was beginning to hurt from smiling. The little chit. She thought she had him by his.... "Yes, government money. It's been allocated."

"How did you find us?" she countered.

"The Fur and Refuge Department in New Orleans gave me the name of a fur buyer. He in turn directed me to you—your father, actually."

"If my papa was alive, he would help you, but—"

"Aren't you your father's daughter?" He gave up all pretense of smiling. It felt wonderful to relax his face.

Patch shot an unreadable glance at her mother. She had always been papa's girl. *Maman* had doted on Rosalina, not letting her help papa as Patch herself had done. She returned her gaze to Cooper, but her eyes were guarded, for he had touched a vulnerable spot in her. "Yes, I am, *m'sieu.*" She was softening, yet fighting every inch of the way. "But look at your manicured hands, free of calluses. You're a city man, unused to swamp living. You wouldn't make it without constant vigilance. You'd hold me back. I camp deep in the swamp during trapping season, only coming in every few weeks or so for supplies and to sell my furs. It's lonely, too." That last just slipped out. Oh, her own tongue, betraying her like that.

Loneliness. The word hung in Cooper's mind. Well, he'd lived his entire life with that. He paused in a curl of smoke, considering an appeal to the mother. Instinct told him that wasn't the right approach, however. Natalie had demanded courtesy from Patch, but in this discussion of business she had deferred to her daughter. Then he stumbled on the truth. The father being dead, the mother crippled, the grandmother old, this dark-eyed girl was the sole support of the family. With his talk of money he was trampling on pride. He knew, because he had his own pride. It kept him whole and it kept him from being hurt. He backtracked, using his most persuasive tone, finding it somehow important that Patch accept him.

"Give it a chance. One week. I'll work alongside of you. After all, the people who live here are part of the environment and are affected by any decisions made back in Washington. You're right about me being a deskman. Show me what it's really like." His blue eyes glittered with appeal while he struck his coup de grace. "If after a week you send me packing, I'll go and find other living quarters, if need be... and no hard feelings."

Patch looked past Cooper, past her mother, out the windows where only blackness filled the void. The beating of her heart thrumbed in her ears, muting music from the radio, the sound of dishes being scraped by *grand-mère* in the kitchen. It wasn't likely that God would exchange Cooper Vachec for a patient man. In the deep swamp she could test his mettle. And there wasn't exactly a jostling queue of men waiting to ask her hand in marriage. To say no would be folly. If later she didn't like him, she could easily rid herself of him.

Her gaze swung from the window to her cup, as if her future lay in dregs of coffee gone cold. Against her will, against all that she believed in, a minute speck of hope, that fodder for dreams, plopped into her hollow soul. She lifted her eyes finally to Cooper's. "All right. I'll take you. The swamp's more subtle in the winter, but just as dangerous," she warned. "Alligators still feed at night, deadly snakes still swim, and it's cold. Bone-chilling cold. Trapping comes first. The season's too short for mistakes and lost time."

There came an audible sigh from Natalie, a lesser one from Cooper. A smile played at the edges of his mouth, deepening the corners. An unexpected warmth enveloped him, and he noticed a slight trembling in his stomach. He put it down to the flush of victory. "You won't regret this, I promise."

Patch was taken by his smile, but not by his words. "Promises?" Her sarcasm was beyond redemption. "From the likes of you, *m'sieu*, one does not accept promises."

2

THE DEAL WAS MADE; the man was hers. Observing Cooper out the corner of her eye, Patch kept to her feet, held erect by that thing in her that all her life had kept her facing squarely all dangers, shame, labels and hurt. She did not acknowledge Cooper excusing himself to get his luggage. But the instant his back turned, her gaze stayed on him until he was out the door, which banged shut on an icy draft.

"You watch yourself," Natalie warned.

"I always do, *maman.*"

Patch slipped back onto the stool as Grand-mère Duval shuffled into the parlor, behaving as though the rest of them did not exist. Her dark eyes followed the old woman with affectionate interest and tolerance. Boarders, *grand-mère* would have them understand, were nothing extraordinary in her life. She lowered herself into her rocker and with a kick of her foot, set it to rocking to and fro.

Grand-mère liked being old. She did not suffer the absence of certain pleasures of the young, and she saw no harm in living in the past. At her age she had more past than future, and it gave her license to see what she wanted and to ignore what she did not. Or pretend to ignore, Patch thought, as *grand-mère* was choosing to do now.

There was nothing wrong with *grand-mère*'s sanity, like some fools were apt to comment. It was just that half a thought often lodged in her brain while the other half found its way to her lips. If *grand-mère*

Beneath a Saffron Sky

suffered a vanity, it was over her teeth. "All my own," she was likely to tell friends and strangers alike, smiling and peering at people through a wrinkled face made leathery by hard years of summer sun and winter cold.

Patch saw her grandmother slyly glower at Natalie from beneath her sunken shuttered lids, as though the younger woman bore a shameful secret or was up to some unnamed villainy. When she was a child, Patch had often thought Grand-mère Duval could read minds, so accurately had the old woman discerned her hidden thoughts.

Now music from the radio caught Grand-mère Duval's attention: "A Closer Walk with Thee" in the Cajun patois. Her heavy wrinkled lids dropped to her cheeks. Planning her journey again, prob'ly. Patch had heard often of that journey, of the great bird with trailing pointed wings that would lead *grand-mère* to Duval, the husband who had tread the path before her, dying in the jungles of Bataan in World War II.

Patch mused for a moment on what shameful thing her mother could have done to cause *grand-mère* to glare at her so. Then it came to her and she swung around on the stool, her mind once again riveted on Cooper Vachec. "Where is he to sleep, *maman*?"

"He can take your bed, no?" Natalie replied. "You sleep with your grandmother. She won't mind."

"M'sieu Vachec is going to mind," predicted Patch with feeling.

Natalie stiffened, delivering a scornful glance. "Is this not my house? It is I who says where one is to sleep."

Patch almost shook with dismay. "You never think things through, *maman*. You know you don't. You plan birthday parties and forget the cake, you make dresses and leave no space for zippers, you invite ten for dinner and cook for six. When papa was alive, we made jokes. We don't have him here to smooth things over now, to make everyone laugh."

"I'm not so adverse to government money as you," said Natalie, her lips twisting. "Rosalina needs another operation. And speaking of money, was fishing good today?"

"Only four hundred pounds. The bayous are too muddy, and the price dropped to fifty cents a pound. The money's in my jacket in the bathroom. But, another operation?" she asked, her heart sinking. "You said the last one would...would.... You've had a letter from the doctors? From Rosalina?"

Natalie's eyes glistened. "No, I called."

"It's been a year...." Sorrow and a guilt-fed anguish underscored Patch's words. She looked at her mother, pleading, "Please, you must talk to Rosalina. I want to see her."

"She refuses, and now you're beginning to sound like Gaston." Natalie's full lips drew into a thin line.

Another surge of guilt washed over Patch. Gaston Voisin was Rosalina's fiancé, and he had not abandoned Rosalina as Arlis had abandoned Patch herself. "She blames me still, no?"

"She says not." Natalie sighed. "She just doesn't want anyone to see her face until...."

Patch rubbed her temple. "Will the doctors make it right this time?"

"I pray so," said Natalie, her expression softening, hopeful. "Ah, here is our boarder...." She turned a charming smile on Cooper as he entered the parlor. "Patch will get you settled in, *m'sieu*. Later, if you like, you can sit here by the fire and listen to the radio. We have a television, but the reception isn't as good as it should be."

"Fine," Cooper said, standing by the door as Patch came toward him. "Lead on," he told her.

A feeling of despair and helplessness subdued Patch. That Rosalina needed yet another operation was a terrible blow. She knew skin grafts were painful, and she hated it that Rosalina had to suffer. Time and money, *maman* said, and eventually all would be well. A feathery sigh escaped her as she canted a sideways look at Cooper. Once he saw the sleeping arrangements, he'd take off like a deer. It was just as well. Her mouth felt suddenly dry. "Bedrooms are across the dogtrot," she said.

As she strode past him he put his hand at the small of her back. Each of his fingers was immediately imprinted on her through the thin shirt, making her legs go weak. She didn't give a thought to her jacket hanging in the bathroom, but choked back a gasp, moving faster than he to put distance between them. When they emerged into the cold wind sweeping through the tunnellike porch he grabbed up his bag.

"In here." She opened the door, snapping on the lights that dangled over each bed. The bare bulbs gave off a harsh glow, revealing a long narrow room with beds at each end, divided at night by a curtain drawn across the center. Just now the thick tapestry hung limply on its ceiling rod against the far wall. Patch felt as limp as the curtain and moved quickly to the heater, squatting to light it before her knees gave way entirely. "You're to take that bed—mine," she said, waving a hand casually toward the end of the room.

Cooper pivoted silently on his heels, his Adam's apple working as though he meant to speak. But nothing that resembled words came forth, only a brief tuneless bark, a laugh. "And that bed at the opposite end of the room?"

"Where I'll sleep with *grand-mère*."

Grand-mère's bed was low to the floor, with feather mattresses. Beside it on the wall was a shrine that held a statue of the Virgin Mary. The tiny shelf was covered with pools of melted wax from sacred candles. There *grand-mère* knelt each night to pray, and when she was having one of her spells, she prayed for the soul of *grand-père*.

Seconds elapsed. Cooper's eyes widened, then narrowed to slits as he realized he'd just agreed to pay board to share a room with two women; one in her dotage who frequently made sentences that had nothing to do with what went before, and...he slanted a look at Patch. He'd been had, and the knowledge made him groan inside. But damned if he let on that it bothered him. "It's clean and it looks comfortable. Nothing to be ashamed of," he elaborated, moving to the window to look out. There was nothing to see. Fog had rolled in, smothering moss-draped cypress and the narrow rut-filled road paved with shells that he had traveled less than two hours earlier. It'd be hell trying to drive into town in that to find a room.

"I'm not ashamed of my room, *m'sieu.*" Patch watched him drag his duffel to her end of the room, his now, and test the bed. It sagged slightly with her imprint. Only this past year, with Rosalina in Baton Rouge, had she had the entire bed to herself. It was covered with thick patchwork quilts and feather pillows stuffed by *grand-mère* long ago.

"I didn't mean that you should be, only I sensed...." There was an upward sweep of his thick brows. "Hell, I don't know what I mean. I'm sure I'll be quite comfortable...."

"*Grand-mère* whiffles, *maman* should have warned you," Patch said.

"Whiffles?" His heart beat heavily, once, twice.

He let his hand drop in resignation. He'd come this far....

"Whiffling is kind of like snoring, not too loud."
She read his expression to say: What else can happen to me?

"Do you whiffle, too?" He was asking sweetly, but his fair eyebrows rose mockingly.

"No one's ever said." The hard incandescent glow from the lights made his blond hair catch fire, and now Patch noticed his complexion was faintly sprinkled with freckles. This intrigued her as much as the shape of his nose and mouth, for few Cajuns were so fair. "I suppose I'll know in the morning, won't I?"

She made an adjustment to the heater, and Cooper caught the outline of her small breasts against the material of her blouse. Part of his brain was telling him he was making a fool of himself, ogling her like he'd just crossed into puberty.

Patch shifted to the wall and pulled the curtain, cutting the room in two. "I have to see if *grand-mère* needs anything," she said, making an excuse to get away from his penetrating gaze. It made her feel undressed to her bones.

"Wait! I.... Who goes to bed first?" Despite the curtain, both beds could be seen by anyone entering or leaving the room.

Patch shrugged. "Whoever is tired, I suppose."
Then she had a thought. God had already made one mistake; He might have made another, one far worse. "Does anyone complain that *you* snore, *m'sieu*?" She couldn't say the word wife, but she was thinking it.

Cooper had a sudden delightful feeling that she wanted to know whether or not he was free. "There's more to you than meets the eye, isn't there?" he bantered.

"I was making a joke," she said icily, giving lie to her words. "We Cajuns have a sense of humor."

He glanced wryly about his half of the room. "So I noticed."

"There are rooms to be had in Catahoula, *m'sieu*." She uttered the words, then felt constrained to hold her breath.

"Did I say I didn't like it here?"

"You're acting like it. This is our home, and my mother has offered you what we have. If it isn't good enough...."

She was making him feel gauche. To combat his sense of discomfiture he found himself telling her, "I lived the first seven years of my life in a root cellar. It was all we had left after a tornado cut across us. Compared to that, this is luxury."

Her gaze was unfaltering, her eyes catching and holding him with their magic. "Do they have tornadoes in Washington?"

"Arkansas."

"We have hurricanes."

"Just as dangerous."

"This house has withstood every one for more than two hundred years."

"Touché, friend," he admitted softly. Then, he added, "Call me Cooper, why don't you?" He was thinking that he liked her eyes in the harsh glare of the overhead bulb; he was less likely to stumble and drown himself in them.

Patch struggled to throw off the inertia that was tugging at her, keeping her rooted to the floor. "If you would like to sit at the kitchen table a few minutes, I'll get *grand-mère* to prayers and bed."

"And afterward?"

Her lids dropped to half-mast. He was casting sensuous innuendos to see where it would get him. She resisted the urge to flaunt her sexuality. "And afterward, I suggest you get a good night's sleep. We'll begin setting up camp tomorrow."

"I'll be ready."

She had her hand on the doorknob.

"No one has complained that I snore," he said, his eyes dancing with a roguish glint.

She went to get her grandmother with a singing heart.

"MAY I JOIN YOU?"

Patch pivoted, nearly losing her grip on the tea-kettle. Her hair was damp from her bath, clinging in tendrils to her nape. She was covered by a soft terry robe, belted at the waist, and a pair of woolen socks on her feet, sturdy nighttime wear that didn't hide the proud lines of her body. "I thought you had gone to bed."

"I couldn't sleep," said Cooper, emerging all the way into the kitchen. He had gone to the parlor first, expecting to find her there.

"I was just making myself a cup of tea. Would you like one?"

"I'd love it." He hated the stuff. As she nodded and turned away for another cup and saucer, he caught an evocative whiff of lavender soap. It summoned an aching need low in his belly.

Patch sensed Cooper's eyes following her every move, felt her skin flaming, growing taut with anticipation. "Sugar, lemon or milk?" she asked, dismayed at the slight quaver in her voice.

"Just plain."

She steeped the tea, poured it, gestured for him to sit. "You can smoke if you want, and if you crave cigarettes, make sure you have enough for camp. If we run out of anything, most prob'ly we'll do without."

"Thanks for the reminder. I've a couple of cartons in my duffel." When Patch nodded and smiled faintly, his gaze slid to her lips. Catching himself

imagining the taste of them, he took a sip of the
tea—and came close to gagging.

"I like mine strong. Is it too bitter for you?"

"It's fine, just went down the wrong pipe." He
gave her a weak smile that didn't quite come off.

"You ever consider doing anything besides government work?" She liked his face, the blondness of
it, the sprinkling of boyish freckles. She didn't like
the kind of work he did, and a woman had to live
with a man's work as much as with his face.

"Not lately. Look, I'm sorry if we got off to a bad
start. I wasn't in the best of moods when I arrived—"

Her intuition was working, stabbing. "Because
you thought you'd come on a wild-goose chase, no?
And found yourself in a house full of women?"

"I don't mind about the women, but I'm not
happy about taking your bed. I can bunk down on
the sofa."

"Not on *maman's* sofa—she'd have a fit."

He made no comment and conversation lagged.
Patch found herself under his scrutiny. She had the
feeling he was appraising her, making up his mind
about something. Her heart began to race. She
moved her cup an inch, and when he didn't follow
the movement, she knew he was lost in an introspection that perhaps had nothing to do with her.
She didn't want to be the first to go to bed, so started
making herself another cup of tea, glancing uneasily
toward him. "What about you?" she offered. "More
tea?"

"No, thanks." Stubbing out his cigarette, he rose
abruptly, as if matters of more importance awaited
him elsewhere.

He'd found an answer to what he'd been worrying about, Patch decided. She sagged a little at the
stove, wondering if he was thinking of leaving. But

he walked to her and squeezed her shoulder, his touch making her skin burn. "Think I'll try that bed again. I'm beat. Thanks for the tea."

He was staying! She was afraid to smile, afraid that her feelings would cover her face. "Good night, *m'sieu*," she called after him in a choked whisper.

Cooper didn't hear, and even if he had, it wouldn't have helped. Her pillow smelled of lavender, robbing him of sleep and peace of mind.

3

THE VOICE OF HER DREAM blurred, faded and sharpened once more to the tapping of a willow twig brushing the pane. Patch stirred, pressing her face into the nubby duck-feather pillow, reluctant to let the exquisite vision pass. Drowsily she huddled among the quilts, but when she came in contact with her grandmother's papery old skin, the dream was gone.

The morning twilight had not yet begun, and her eyes, wide with the dark, searched out the shadows of the room. She could not see the others, but by their breathing she knew that they were asleep: *grand-mère* by her side, Cooper in her own bed on the other side of the curtain.

Life was full of beginnings and endings. Birth and death she discounted, because no one escaped either. It was all the little ones that kept her distracted. Cooper Vachec's coming was a beginning.... The willow twig brushed the pane again, giving off a tinny sound. All the sap had gone down to its roots, she thought. All of her own sap was in her roots, too. Boiling there. Cooper Vachec had set it to full rising.

The horizon was paling. Patch sat upright and swung her feet onto the floor. She wanted to have a look at him, sleeping in her bed—the impulse came swiftly. She bent down, gathering up her robe, and on bare feet moved across the room. She was disappointed, for there was little to see in the gray gloom of dawn. Cooper slept on his stomach, one arm crooked above his head, which was buried in the lavender-scented pillow.

A sudden sense of guilt washed over Patch. She had a savage need to be desired, to be cherished, to have a helpmate in the harsh life she lived. But she had promised Rosalina, had given her word that she herself would not marry until Rosalina was well enough to take her own marriage vows. It had seemed such a small thing to pledge then, with her sister cradled in her arms after the accident. She did not regret the comfort her vow had given to Rosalina that awful day. She didn't!

A fluttering drew her attention to the window. A lone heron lifted gracefully from the levee, robbing the dawn of its solitude. The bird soared effortlessly against a fitful icy wind that stirred willows and set moss to swaying. Patch watched with a twinge of envy. The only flying she did was in her mind, and that was a flight of fancy.

She looked once more at the sleeping form of Cooper, marveling at his wide shoulders, the thatch of wiry curls, not unlike her own. He might prove out, she thought, might be a patient man. Monsignor Burns, the old priest who had taught her catechism, had told her that God sees all, knows all, even wicked thoughts. But most prob'ly, Patch thought sincerely, God was too tasteful and mannerly to inquire into that part of her brain making plans for the seduction of Cooper Vachec. Still, she glanced swiftly over her shoulder, but there was no one to notice that she was on the road to perdition.

The day was fully light when, a little self-consciously because Cooper's eyes were on her, Patch held out her hand to her grandmother. "Tell my fortune, *grand-mère*."

The old woman ran a gnarled, still-facile finger over Patch's palm, gently tracing the calluses raised there. "What do you want to know for? It stays the same, no?"

"No it doesn't, it changes."

"Never. What your fate is set up to do, it does."

"That's not what you told Father Burns."

"Bah! All he believes in is sin. Results are same, no? Just the paths are different. Sin is the invention of man, but fate is God's province, much more practical than sin."

"You see something bad there, don't you? That's why you won't tell me?"

The old woman withdrew her hand, looked slyly at Cooper and sipped her coffee. "I see wishful thinkin'...." The rivers of wrinkles in her face bunched up, and she smiled brilliantly to show off her teeth. "More than one soul's trailing the great white bird. That's your fortune." Then her hooded eyes stared off into space.

"*Gran*—" Patch checked herself for the old woman had excluded her. She sighed and turned to Cooper.

He wore a gray turtleneck sweater, jeans and leather boots, expensive-looking like all his things. Even his after-shave smelled of money. Her own red sweater was laddered at both elbows, her thick wool pants had been mended more than once at the knee. She ought to keep back some trapping money for herself, she thought, buy up some new clothes. Lipstick, perfume, too. Immediately she felt mean and guilty, for all the money was needed by Rosalina. No sense trying to keep up with government money. But she had to admit she found Cooper unparalleled in refinement.

"Finish your breakfast," she ordered with a trace of annoyance when he stretched and yawned like a lion. "I don't want to know right off that you're a slacker."

"It's barely dawn," he protested lightly. "I'm no

good until I've had plenty of coffee and a morning smoke."

"If you're coming out to camp with me—"

He grinned. "You're too tiny to behave like a bully."

"I'm not as big as you are, that's sure," she said succinctly, miffed because more than anything she wanted to appear womanly, disarming and desirable.

"Be with you in a few minutes," he said, reaching for the coffeepot.

She was seeing a stubbornness in him that she recognized, though in herself she called it determination. In an indescribable way she was beginning to sense that she had met her match. "It's cold out on the bog. Did you bring lots of warm underwear?" she asked, changing tack.

"I brought a pair of long johns."

"I'll pack you some of papa's. 'Thout a change you'll be smelling higher than the skinning shed." The sun was poking through a break in the mist, promising light but no warmth. She put her cup on the sink counter. "I'll be in the sheds out back."

She left him sitting at the table with *grand-mère*, liking him on a different level because he didn't seem to take offense at the old woman's ways.

"THAT BOAT LOOKS OLDER than Methuselah—like maybe it was built by Noah as a dinghy," complained Cooper, wearing a worried frown that made the grooves on each side of his nose deepen. Sweat beaded his upper lip despite the biting cold. He and Patch had been working steadily for hours stowing gear: blankets, clothes, food, drums of fuel, ice, a hoop net that Patch said would provide them with suppers. He handed her a last box tied with cord and watched her wedge it carefully between a drum of diesel fuel and a tank of propane. The boat lay precariously low in the water.

"It's older than me anyway," Patch told him.

He put his hands on his hips, blue eyes alight behind stubby blond lashes. "How old is that?"

"Twenty-three."

"You don't look a day over fifteen."

He thought that because she didn't have any bosom; she just knew it. It had been on the tip of her tongue to ask his own age, but she wouldn't now for the world. She guessed thirty, but you couldn't tell with city people. Protected from the elements, their skin stayed too smooth. She angled a look up at him on the pier. "This boat served my papa well, and now it serves me. Stow your duffel and get in. We must make camp before dark."

Cooper stalled. "I agreed to help you, not to drown." He was somewhat piqued. Patch had been ordering him about all day. "Hold that pulley... pack this...get that from the shed. Give your car keys to *maman* for safekeeping...undo that, you've got it all wrong." He didn't like taking orders from a woman.

"I won't let you drown, *m'sieu.* I promise. You're much too valuable." Her clear dark eyes seemed to pick up tiny lights.

"Suppose I think the same of your promises that you do of mine?"

The irony in his tone made her glance sharply at him. "Well, you shouldn't," she replied with a woman's logic that eluded Cooper.

"Tell me this, then. What makes me so valuable?" He kind of liked being thought valuable and felt a sudden warmth envelop him.

"All in good time, *m'sieu,*" she said, and the lights in her eyes dimmed mysteriously. "Please hurry, every moment of daylight counts against mishap."

Caustic by nature, Cooper admitted he was a bit hasty to temper, insolent to the point of rebellion, and often arrogant. It was all a facade to mask a vulnerability he wouldn't admit even to himself. If he had ever been truly loved, he didn't know it. What he did know was that he had, with his eyes wide open, committed himself to live and work for the next weeks alongside an elfin creature called Patch. Last night his dreams had been filled with sloe-eyed maidens who had small upthrusting breasts and beckoning smiles. His loins still ached from the unfulfilling dream, but the warmth he felt now erased the sharpness from his retort.

"You're a regular little Napoleon, you know that?" He tossed his duffel onto the wooden box that held ice and stepped into the boat, wincing as it sank deeper into the water.

Patch was brisk, all business as Cooper settled himself on the opposite side of the tiller. She glanced at him once, but when their eyes met she looked quickly away. She had never been more aware of a man in her life. The skin bracer he used had a woodsy smell unlike anything she'd ever known in the swamp. During the day she'd worked as near to him as she dared just so she could get an occasional whiff. Now the cold wind that cut across the bayou filled her nostrils with its heady scent. She closed her eyes, inhaling. "The air's soft today," she said dreamily.

Cooper reached across the tiller, touching her arm. Her eyes flew open. "Are you worried about anything?" he asked.

"Just praying for a safe journey," she improvised, while the contours of her cheeks flamed with color.

Cooper eyed the water lying inches below the high sides of the boat. "That's not a bad idea."

Patch started the motor. It caught at once, and the

steady throbbing drew Natalie to the dogtrot. Patch
gave a wave, threw off the mooring lines and turned
the laden thirty-foot skiff into a deep canal.

She maneuvered around submerged stumps, sandbars and shallows, guiding them through a labyrinth
of islands with consummate skill. She spent most of
the time on her feet, with just her fingertips on the
tiller. Her eyes were narrowed against the wind, her
face in repose, belying the wonderful tempest that
raged within her.

To Cooper the air smelled of wet sea and tropical
mud gone cold. Patch pointed out spoil banks left by
the dredgers, an oil well, a rookery or a trapper's
camp. He made mental notes of what she told him,
shrugging deeper into his fleece-lined coat and
keeping a wary eye on the water sloshing about in
the bottom of the boat.

Yet again and again his gaze was drawn to Patch.
As they moved deeper into the swamp she seemed to
meld with the landscape, becoming a part of its es-
sence. He could feel the change in her. It was nothing you could put your hand on; an intensification
of all that she was. It was an aura of earthiness, a
shift in her manner as though now she were on na-
tive land. Cooper found himself entranced.

A hard breeze was pouring down the bayou. Now
and again they passed behind a high island that
acted as a windbreak and the relief was stupendous.
During one of these lulls he tried to talk to Patch
about her metamorphosis.

She turned her great somber eyes on him. A stirring in her nerves was creating a strangeness in
her, making a tinderbox of her thighs. "Monsignor
Burns says I'm a wild thing, a throwback. But here
one survives on instinct, finely tuned. In town the
noises all confuse me, all of them so crushed atop
one another. Here—" she waved a hand, a delicate

slice through air "—sounds are layered. The owl calls at night, bull alligators roar, cotton rats squeak, gulls chatter, bucks rut and have favorite trees to rub the cotton from their antlers. Natural sounds, each distinct, that don't clash. In town the people confuse me, too, and I make mistakes. In the swamp, never."

As she talked Cooper's thoughts flew to the accustomed frenzy of Washington. Cocktail parties with overdressed men and underdressed women packed into a small space. Loud music, cigarette smoke, everyone talking at once and nobody listening. He understood what Patch was saying, but the world she didn't like was the one in which he functioned best.

She maneuvered the boat around a bent old cypress, limbs outthrust like a priest administering last rites. He pulled out a cigarette, cupped his hands and lit it. "Never?" he asked.

Patch paused, thinking of Arlis Lafargue. "Once." The reply was a dry whisper. She had been chasing a rainbow and lost track of it somehow. It had changed her life forever.

They came out from behind the island and the wind kicked up wet spume. Patch was aware of a quickening between herself and the man beside her, a humming as if something long dormant was beginning to come alive. She didn't know if it was good or bad, and buried her chin in the scratchy warmth of her collar.

An unbidden sense of protectiveness for Patch was washing over Cooper. The emotion, one long suppressed, made a memory surface. His mother had had that knack of making him feel big and strong.

His expression went hard. Somehow the girl was making him feel that way on purpose. Resolutely he turned his gaze back to the water, letting himself be mesmerized, as if some elusive answer hid in the churning black lace folding away from the prow.

PATCH CUT THE MOTOR, and in the sudden silence the old skiff nosed up to the sturdy wharf as if it knew it was home. The swamp hummed of vague rustlings, slitherings, odd croaks, whistlings and the hushed whisper of threat. "We're here, *m'sieu*," she told Cooper. "And we suffered no mishaps, yes?" She turned to give him what she hoped was an entreating smile, only to discover a harsh frown of worry creasing his brow. She didn't know it, but she was looking into the face of panic.

Cooper was not an adventurer. He had physical strength and dexterity and had acquired a certain amount of sophistication during two years in college and three years in the military. He had beat out more experienced applicants for his job with the EPA due to points the civil service gave to veterans, then had inadvertently given to a hostile reporter an uncomplimentary interview that got him fired. But he liked the job, and setting himself up as a freelance environmental investigator, he got all the work he wanted or could handle.

He liked solid earth beneath his feet. He had been raised on a farm, where water was something you bathed in or drank and mud was something you did not track onto carpets. Now he was surrounded by a sea of each. Up until this moment, working with Patch Chauvin had seemed a lark.

Camp was a tar-paper shack on stilts propped upon a small spit of bog. A rain barrel canted perilously on spindly legs, buttressed against a south-facing wall. Under the shack were a belly-up pirogue, a shallow-draft skiff and several bundles of cane poles. There were outbuildings and sheds, some on stilts while others hugged the soft earth as if waiting for it to swallow them up. Back of the shack as far as the eye could see were scrub trees draped with the ever-present moss, muddy canals and endless miles of swamp grass.

The dismay on his face drove Patch to speech. "What's wrong, *m'sieu*? Are you sick? The swaying of the boat, perhaps?"

His lips twisted slightly. "Looks...lonesome," he said, then voiced his worst fear. "A man could die out here, and no one would ever know."

"Oh, yes we would," she assured him. "If a man fell out of his boat, it would float free and raise questions. If he went out to trap in the morning and was bitten by a snake and didn't return to camp, his partner would sound an alarm. But of course, if he were eaten by an alligator, we might not know until the alligator was caught and skinned. Then we'd find his watch or some such in the stomach. So you see—oh lor! *m'sieu*! You've gone so pale—here, take my arm."

"I'm perfectly well," said Cooper tightly, pleased with the steadiness of his voice.

But there was in his control something that triggered Patch's instincts, and she discerned his fear. "You mustn't worry," she crooned. "Nothing is going to happen to you, except that which God has ordained."

"I don't get the feeling He hangs around here very much," Cooper said glumly, regarding her appealing little moue with overt suspicion. In his loins was a tangible sense of unease.

Patch's hand dropped to her side, a graceful delicate thing despite the calluses and short squared nails. "Don't blaspheme so, *m'sieu*," she said crossly. "You could ruin everything!"

Her declaration of piety was the only genuine article of faith Cooper had seen in years. He paused.

Probably prays over her traps, he thought, remembering the candles and statue in the bedroom. He
glanced once more at the shack, the moss-covered
stumps, the soupy mud where all manner of poisonous creatures undoubtedly lurked. He hoped
he'd see his thirty-fourth birthday. "Sorry," he said
finally, and with a care he would never have displayed crossing a busy street, hauled himself onto
the dilapidated-looking wharf.

Together they began the laborous task of unloading the boat. Winches had to be applied to haul up
the drums of fuel, and muscle to roll them up the
wharf. Ropes had to hold them against mishap on a
ledge at the back of the shack. The night was chill
and cloudless, the sky deepening to a more velvety
black by the time they turned their energies to inside
the camp.

The screen on the rain barrel was cleaned, water
level checked. "Low," Patch said. "We'll have to use
bayou water for dishes and bathing." While Cooper
held a flashlight, she pumped diesel fuel into a small
generator that provided electricity to the single bulb
over a dining table. The propane tank was hooked
up to copper pipes that fueled the refrigerator. Patch
lighted the pilot light, set the temperature, then
tuned to Cooper with a smile. "We can't put food
into it until it gets cold, but we're almost settled,
no?"

The camp was one room, a repository for castoffs.
It smelled of mud and raw leather, not unpleasant to
Cooper's nose, just different. Having four walls
about him gave him a euphoric sense of safety. A
window in each wall reflected the single bulb dan-
gling over the table, which was host to four mis-
matched chairs. At opposite ends of the room were
double bunks, and a sofa, its springs intact, held
court in the middle of the floor. With the door open,

as it was now, the sofa's occupants could see any
traffic on the canal. Deer antlers hung near front
and back doors held rain gear, old jackets, knit caps.

Patch hung her guns in the rack next to her bunk,
then went to an old Chilkoot icebox, serving now as
a cabinet. Lifting the lid, she took out a candle and a
small wooden statue of St. Joseph. Lighting the
candle, she knelt and bent her head in silent
prayer.

Cooper watched with a spark of embarrassment.
He was intrigued with the hand-carved statue, for
he was an avid collector of wood sculptures. He
studied it until she traced the sign of the cross on her
forehead and rose to her feet.

"That was for papa—I know he misses trapping.
Now I'll begin supper." And a fine supper it would
be; Cooper ought to find out that she could cook. A
man might be off anywhere, drinking, playing cards
with cronies, but when his stomach began to grum-
ble with hunger, he'd point his feet where he knew
hot tasty food awaited him.

She made a meal of Blue Runner Creole beans, rice
and fried chicken. She knew Cooper was watching
her, and what his thoughts might be she didn't
know. But she knew her own. She meant to find out
how he had spent every minute of his life before
God had placed him on her doorstep. Information
was vital. One did not plan a seduction of the magnitude she had in mind—the results being marriage—without first gathering critical intelligence.
No officer planning a battle would do less. As her
mind raced forward in anticipation her breasts began to hum. Growing, Patch hoped.

During dinner she plied him with questions.
"Where were you born?" she began.

"Arkansas."

"Where that root cellar was?"

"Where the root cellar was."

"And your parents?"

Cooper scowled. "Dead. The same tornado that took our house killed my dad and my older brother."

"And your mother, *m'sieu*?"

Cooper stiffened visibly. He had been abandoned in childhood by his mother and the memory of that hurt, and loneliness was like a second self. He deflected Patch's question. "What happened to your dad?"

"Drowned last year, just before trapping season." She sensed his reticence to discuss his mother, but was not to be put off. "Where do you live? In Washington, I mean."

"A garage apartment. My landlady's the widow of a former aide to an ambassador to France."

Patch lifted eyes filled with intensity to Cooper's tactile blue ones. "Is she very beautiful?"

One golden eyebrow lifted in amusement. "Yes."

"Does she do your laundry, cook for you, clean behind you?" Patch asked with carefully camouflaged concern, trying to find something that would set herself apart from the beautiful landlady.

"None of those things," Cooper said with a grin, spearing another piece of chicken.

"What a useless woman," she sniffed. She put her plate in the sink, opened the front door and leaned against the jamb, arms folded, looking out into the night.

The single bulb lit her sable curls, the slight curve of her shoulders, her straight spine, the snug-fitting wool pants that delineated perfectly formed hips and legs. Cooper stared at her freely, captured by her stillness.

She turned to look at him once, her expression grave. He sensed her thoughts, yet couldn't grasp them. He felt in that moment her passion; that they were linked in a subtle exchange. But what that exchange was remained as elusive as answers he'd sought in the lacy waves off the boat's prow. Shaken, he got up and rummaged through his duffel for a carton of cigarettes.

"What are the women like in Washington?" she asked suddenly, breaking the stillness. "Besides your landlady."

"Like women everywhere," he answered with some derision. "Hard in some ways, easy in others, painted with lipstick and eyebrow goo."

Patch frowned, registering his dislike of paint, and struck lipstick from her mental shopping list.

A THOUSAND SPIDERS spinning gossamer webs in her stomach, that's what it felt like, Patch thought as she stood over Cooper. It seemed unreasonable that having just met him she should take such joy in watching him breathe in and out, but she did. Two days was plenty for her to know her mind, and for him, too. She'd been able to tell yesterday—the way his eyes measured her, sending decisive messages. Now he was making soft snuffling wake-up noises that made the gossamer webs pull tight like they were going to shred.

All night long she had tossed and wrested with a problem. Should she or should she not open her mouth when Cooper kissed her. Should, she had decided as the first pale light of dawn crept through the uncurtained windows, or else a kiss wouldn't be worthwhile. She had never let Arlis put his tongue in her mouth. What with him chewing tobacco and all, it hadn't seemed sanitary.

She moved lightly, like a wisp of fog, back to her side of the shack. As she pulled on cords and a flannel shirt over skintight thermal underwear, a strong incalculable tug kept her glancing at Cooper. Now that she had decided about their kissing, she wanted him to wake up and get on with it.

In the thin light his hair was a golden color, awry now, and she longed to run her fingers through it. When his lids began to flutter, she turned to her tasks—boiling water for coffee, for bathing face and hands. After she started bacon frying, she opened the front door to let in an umber gold-flecked light. Fuel was precious, the generator switched on only at full dark. Soon her neck began to prickle, and she knew she was being watched.

"Is it morning already?" came Cooper's voice, seductive in a lazy, languorous stage of awakening.

The tone of his voice set the tone for her answer. She said throatily, "Yes, *m'sieu*," considering for a moment serving him breakfast in bed. But no, the camp was a place of work, not coddling. He needed to know that.

There was an echo of a smile on his lips. "Are you ever going to call me Cooper?"

"Of course, *m'sieu*." She moved to the stove and cracked eggs into a warm skillet, discovering her hands were shaking. Every yoke split wide open. "Do you like scram—" she began, casting a backward glance over her shoulder.

He was standing by his bunk, naked, yawning and stretching, his muscles rippling from corded neck to.... Patch couldn't tear her eyes away, didn't want to. Beard stubble was thick on his jaw, a thick mat of coppery hair on his chest, fine pale down on his legs.... She felt her mouth going dry.

His arms came down out of the stretch, his eyes opened, met hers and widened. Mortified, she spun around to the stove.

"I thought you said ground rules were word of honor not to peek," he said derisively. In fact, her startled innocent confusion flattered his male consciousness more profoundly than any soft sensual come-on might have. "Or did you just mean that I wasn't supposed to?"

Patch was beating the eggs so furiously they could

have made a ten-inch souffle. Throughout her body, nerve endings were singing. "You shouldn't sleep naked in camp. It's dangerous—"

"That kind of danger I can handle," he said dryly, coming to the table as he buttoned his shirt.

She spattered egg onto a plate, added bacon, a slice of bread, and put it before him. Her huge dark eyes seemed all pupil. "I understand your innuendo and that's not the kind of danger I mean." But of course, it was. She tossed her head, making her sleep-tousled curls bobble. "Besides, I've seen naked men before."

She endured his grin, the mocking glint in his eyes. "Oh," he said slyly. "And how do I compare?"

Patch swallowed, keenly feeling his question to be a violation of etiquette. He wasn't supposed to think himself better than other men until she told him so. She weighed the meaning of his words, then smiled sweetly. "A bit small in the thighs, *m'sieu*."

His fingers shot out and grasped her wrist, forcing her to look at him, at his laughing blue eyes, his crooked smile. "On top of everything else, you're an accomplished little liar."

He became aware that his fingers encircled her fragile wrist, and that it was trembling. It wasn't much, but his flesh was against her flesh, and he could smell faintly provocative traces of lavender. A primitive lust exploded inside him so that heady images billowed in his mind. He visualized her naked, astride him in delight. He tried to shake loose the pictures from his mind. It was utterly stupid to be thinking of sex with her. "I might not feel so honor bound to look the other way in the future," he said furiously, pulling himself together.

Patch saw the sudden light in his blue eyes, and its prompt extinction. "You're still an arrogant government man." She jerked her wrist free and looked at him steadily. "And I ain't met a one yet what knew his place."

"A job's a job. As for being arrogant, you've got it all over me." He had himself in hand now. "Did you know your eyes change color when you get snippy?"

Lor! Vanity swelled within her at the fact that he had noticed. "Slicked-tongue flattery will get you nowhere."

"I was just making small talk."

"That's what I mean," she said, stabbing at eggs on her plate. She could listen to him say pretty things about her all day. "You city men aren't sincere about anything, no?"

This wasn't going at all like she'd hoped. She had acres and acres of chitchat, but that could wait. The important stuff had to be gotten out of the way first. She drew in her breath sharply. "Since you seem to have sex so high on your mind, have you ever taken up with a woman, *m'sieu*?"

His fork stopped in midair; his gaze turned sharp and predatory like a hawk spotting the tiniest movement of prey. "Taken up?"

She explained in a rapid half whisper. "Been in love."

"No, I haven't, and I don't expect to be, not in the near future. Not ever, come to think of it."

She had an odd sense of buoyancy near her heart, but was careful to betray no emotion. Her brows were dark and straight over the shimmering pools of her eyes. "Why not? You haven't picked a woman you want, or you have and she doesn't want you?"

At his worst when trying to behave in a footloose-and-fancy-free manner, Cooper took unnaturally quick sips of coffee, trying to drown his irritation. "Something lacking, I suppose. I don't like getting involved. I learned long ago that women aren't....

What kind of talk is this?'' he finished, wanting to deflect the topic.

"Just small talk, *m'sieu,*" she said airily, contemplating him for a moment. Her heart sagged as she wondered about his relationship with his beautiful landlady.

"I manage nicely without falling in love, thank you," he said with melodramatic scorn, pressing his well-shaped lips together. "Pass the cream."

"How do you know, if you haven't been involved?" She managed the indifference in her voice with difficulty.

Cooper looked at her with faint surprise. She was getting under his skin, poking around in places she shouldn't, making him think about things well buried. She was coming too close to the man he was, too close to the hurt he had suffered. "Love 'em and leave 'em is my philosophy."

But she had seen a memory taking shape behind his eyes, one that troubled him, and she advanced with unerring clarity. "A woman stomped your feelings once, no?"

He turned away from her to look out the open door, staring for a minute at the play of pale sunlight on dew-wet swamp grass. Trails of vaporous fog rising like smoke gave the swamp the appearance of a steaming black earth. Some of the savagery of the landscape found its way into his voice. "My feelings are none of your business."

Patch sat facing him, knowing that she had touched on a thing buried, a thing hurtful. She chewed thoughtfully on her lower lip. There was more than government to be wrested from Cooper Vachec.

He mopped up the eggs with the last crust of bread, drained his coffee and moved away from the table toward his duffel. "I'd better review the hydrographic charts I brought, map out some sort of grid to work from."

With an inward sigh Patch rose from the table and pushed back her hair with both hands. "I'll clear the table for you to work on."

Dishes didn't get washed until after the last meal of the day, but she set them to soaking in the dishpan.

"I'll be outside if you need me or have any questions," she said, thinking that their first breakfast together in camp had been an undramatic failure. "You can keep a burner on the stove lit to chase off the cold."

He muttered something inarticulate and the feeling heightened. Love was building her, she thought, and sooner or later she'd come on a way to get around him. She held on to the thought as she shrugged into her jacket and went out the door, leaving it open behind her as he'd need the light to work his papers.

Outside, she forgot Cooper for the moment. The cold winter wind was filled with the smell of musty moss and damp leaf mold. Lor, but she would live in camp year-round if the government didn't snoop like they did and catch her at it. If she had the money to haul a barge up from Houma and put a house on it, she could anchor it right there on the bayou. Wasn't anything they could do about that; barges weren't permanent dwellings. She picked out a spot for a garden, a chicken coop, a new rain barrel. She held on to the dream doggedly for several seconds, then gave it up for reality, and pulled on her cotton work gloves.

All must be in readiness for Sunday, the beginning of the season. Rosalina would not get the needed operation until a cash deposit was paid to the hospital and doctor. It was always the way. Even had it been offered, the Chauvins were too proud to accept charity. For an instant Patch felt bowed by the responsibility that was hers alone. She shrugged the feeling off. She'd manage somehow; she always had. There was a good living to be made trapping and fishing if a person wasn't lazy, and she had never been faulted as a layabout. She thought to call Cooper outside and tell him about the barge, but she gave that over, too. She was getting ahead of her dreams. Kissing was one thing, talking like he was staying on permanently was another. Rosalina must be made well first.

Patch worked like a dervish, airing and cleaning the drying sheds, tagging poles to mark the location of traps, sorting and scraping rust off the traps themselves, counting out two hundred of the best. Then she set up the old metal drum, its welded legs on slabs of wood, over the boggy ground, filled it with peanut oil and got a blaze going beneath it. She worked by rote, not thinking, for if she did....

The *putt-putt* of a motor drew her from this task, and Cooper from his charts. He came to the door with a coffee cup in his hand. "I hear a boat," he said conversationally. "Are we getting company?"

"This canal's like a highway. It's the only one deep enough for heavy draft this end of all the leases. Other trappers'll be coming along the next few days going to their camps." She strolled over to the wharf to see who it might be, watching the boat and its occupants come into sharp focus. "It's Indian Jack and his woman. He's going to stop." She waved for Cooper to come down to the wharf as the Indian idled the motor and eased up next to her own boat.

Indian Jack kept a mailbox in Catahoula and lived in the swamp year-round on a houseboat. He had a garden and chickens. Standing still, he took on the shape and color of an old cypress stump. He had four good teeth and kept his long hair braided and colored—black mostly, but sometimes the dye came up purple. He could out trap and hunt any three men in the swamp and had a way with a knife that kept anyone from calling him a sissy for dyeing his hair. His woman was square-built and stoic. Patch had never heard her speak.

"That the government man?" Indian Jack asked, eyeing Cooper up and down.

"Not the badge kind," Patch replied, leaping to Cooper's defense.

Indian Jack nodded, showering her with a four-tooth smile. "Missed you and your pa last season. Ain't nobody could play dominos like Pierre."

"I missed being here."

"Sorry to hear of your sister. She comin' along?"

"She is," said Patch tersely. She didn't want questions raised in Cooper's mind about Rosalina—not yet. She'd do the telling when the time was ripe.

Cooper had put on a plaid wool shirt over the one he'd come to the table buttoning up. He looked elegant again. She introduced him to Indian Jack.

The old man hesitated before thrusting out a stumpy, brown hand.

"Not a badge man, eh?"

Patch stood back so Cooper could speak for himself now. Indian Jack was sizing him up. "A sample man," Cooper said, keeping his hand out. "Just taking water and mud samples to check out pollution."

"*Allô*, then, no?" Indian Jack accepted his hand. Patch sighed. "I know a soil bank's got water so high behind it, crawfish climb out on stumps to get breathing air."

"I'll check it out," Cooper promised.

"Might take ye myself," replied Indian Jack, satisfied Cooper wouldn't be poking into other people's business. He turned to Patch, saying, "You cooking Christmas dinner this year?"

"Reckon I am."

"Blackberry dumplings, no?" He smacked his lips.

"If somebody brought me a mess of flounder to stuff, I'd ask him to stay for blackberry dumplings."

"I'll git the old woman to set a gris-gris on 'em to be sure they take my bait." He started up the idling motor, aimed the craft into the middle of the bayou and with a wave, sailed away.

"He liked you," Patch said to Cooper.

"Is that important?"

She lifted her sweet stern little face, vivid with the story she was going to tell him. "A while back an engineer tried to force Indian Jack off his lease, and once a poacher bragged he'd inroaded old Jack's traps. It was a while later they both came up missing."

"So?" Cooper said indulgently. Seeing her eyes aflame, he decided he'd been too hard on her at breakfast.

"They're still missing, no?"

It was a roundabout message, that story, but Cooper got it. He made himself a promise that he meant to keep. Suffocating crawfish or no, he wouldn't go anywhere with Indian Jack.

"What are you staring at?" he accused, catching Patch's heavy-lidded gaze on him.

Her heart filled with warmth as she looked at him. In her mind she touched him, his smooth face, the knobby chin and his blond curls, his shoulders—other places. Oh, she was heavy with love, willing him to kiss her. "I was just admiring your clothes," she stated.

She was flattering him, and he had the craziest urge to preen. "Thank you." He shoved his hands in his pockets and went back into the shack.

Patch watched him go. If she could recapture the mood he'd been in that first night in her bedroom, he'd be in a kissing mood. But no solution came to her and she, too, went back to work.

Later there was more traffic on the bayou. Trappers *allô*'d and kept on, anxious, Patch knew, to reach their camps. But one heavily laden boat, motor sputtering, chugged up to the camp. From under the shack where she was oiling a motor, Patch noticed who it was. Arlis Lafargue! And he was dragging Una with him. Oh, lor! Arlis was the last person in the world she wanted Cooper to meet. He was too loose-mouthed; he could ruin everything.

Arlis cut the motor and eased up to the wharf, forcing Patch to acknowledge them. She couldn't help her envy of Una, or the humiliation she felt at Arlis's flaunting his relationship with the other woman. The long and short of it was that he had jilted her, and the whole world knew.

' "*Allô*, Patch!" He grinned up at her from the boat.

She felt defiant and resented the feeling. "You have your nerve, Arlis Lafargue!"

"Nature's pressing at Una. She couldn't wait until we made camp."

Una's dark flyaway hair was held in place by a scarf knotted beneath a pinched face. She was bundled up against the cold, but none of the layers of shirts or coat could be buttoned over her protruding belly. A simple, clumsy woman, she was forever apologizing. This as much as anything irritated Patch. Had Arlis left her for someone better, more attractive, she could've just survived on jealousy. It was hard to be mean to Una.

"I'm sorry to run in on you like this, Patch, but Arlis insisted." She didn't meet Patch's glare. "Don't know how much help I'll be to Arlis at camp in the shape I'm in," she added as she struggled to climb out of the boat.

"Keep me warm at night, no?" he replied with another of his wide grins. Patch ignored Arlis and offered Una a helping hand onto the wharf.

"You know where the outhouse is, Una," she said crisply, not turning as she lumbered off.

Arlis eyed Cooper standing in the door of the camp. "Heard you'd hired yourself some help, no?" he said.

"Might have," Patch said stiffly. "Whatever I do is no business of yours anymore."

"Aw, Patch, you're not still mad at me, no? We can still run our leases together, trap together, if you want. Una's not going to be much help in the marsh."

"You should have thought of that before you took up with her, Arlis Lafargue. And stay off my lease. I'll do my own trapping, my own skinning. I don't need any help from you."

He frowned. "You are still mad, no? I wisht you'd understand how it is to be a man. I couldn't help it with Una. She come on to me—"

"Who's your friend?" Cooper asked, coming up behind Patch and putting an arm around her waist as if he owned her. She swallowed hard on a wave of panic, leaning into his arm. He had shaved and the fragrance of his after-shave filled her nostrils. The feel of his arm about her was wonderful.

"Arlis Lafargue has the next lease over," she said, making introductions, and felt a loss when Cooper bent down to reach Arlis's outstretched hand.

"Ah, Patch," Una said as she rejoined them. "You wouldn't have an extra block of ice, would you? We didn't have no time to git into town...."

"I can spare one," she agreed, fuming inwardly. If Cooper hadn't been standing there, she would've refused. She didn't mind helping a neighbor, but one of Arlis's faults was that he was always borrowing. Arlis was weak, she realized suddenly, like water that takes the shape of anything you put it in. Funny how she could see that now. He was getting Una to do his asking for him. She waited for him to say some cataclysmic things that would tell Cooper he had been her intended. But Cooper volunteered to get the fifty-pound block of ice from the box in the shed where it was stored and relief drained through her.

He returned with it balanced upon his shoulder. "There's plenty more, if you run out," he told Arlis.

Patch had to bite her tongue to keep from yelling at him until Arlis and Una were on their way again, then she turned on him like a shrew. "You have your nerve, no? Offering my supplies to that no-good. If you hadn't been here, I wouldn't even have given him that. Did you see him offer to pay? No!"

"Don't get so worked up over a piece of ice." Cooper was taken aback by her vehemence. He reached into his pocket, pulling out a wad of bills, stripping off a few. "Here, I'll be glad to—"

Insulted, she ignored the money. "Arlis just stopped by to rub Una in my face, and you had to make it seem like...like.... Oh!" she gasped. Getting angry like that mixed her up. The relief that she'd felt melted away in one long unsteady breath.

"Is Lafargue something special to you?" he asked, discovering he wouldn't like it if she said yes.

Throwing up her hands in disgust, Patch stalked back into the camp, leaving Cooper glaring after her.

She warmed coffee, and poured herself a cup with trembling hands. When Cooper didn't follow her inside to beg her forgiveness like he ought to, she glided to the door to find he was stooping down, feeding wood to the fire under the oil.

There was a trick of sunlight. It retrieved from a buried nook in her mind the horrible accident that had shattered and reshaped her life. Patch's heart gave a fearsome lurch. Rosalina was trying to shove a log beneath the boiling oil.

The coffee cup slid from her fingers, and she heard herself screaming "No!" But the scream was only in her head because her throat had closed off, blocking her voice.

She went barreling toward Rosalina, arms outthrust, pushing her out of the way and oh, dear God, this time she was on time. This time....

She crashed into Cooper's chest with so much momentum that he was knocked off balance and they both went down, Cooper landing on his back with the breath knocked from his lungs, Patch sprawled across him, her arms and legs still pumping.

Cooper's reflexes were like lightning. He grabbed her shoulders, holding her against him, stilling her with no pretense at gentleness while he gasped for air. "What the hell? Are you crazy? Coming at me like that with no warning—"

Rosalina was safe, the accident nothing more than a bad dream...no, not Rosalina, Cooper. The disappointment was choking. Her eyes clouded with confusion.

She began to tremble and dropped her head to Cooper's chest, one part of her brain cataloging the sensation of lying atop him head to toe, the other aware of the knot of humiliation curdling in her stomach. She struggled to recover, to apologize. "I'm sorry, *m'sieu*," she croaked.

"I'm sorry, *m'sieu*," he mimicked, emulating her lilting voice exactly. "Why in hell did you do that?"

Her knees and thighs were pressing against his; belt buckle, shirt buttons and ribs cut into her stomach and breasts, piercing through the surface to a hidden center of want and need. The barrage of sensations—fear, relief, discovery—were too much. Patch began to sob. "Oh, it was awful...awful...."

Anger to Cooper was nectar; he could wallow in it. Words of love or of anguish made him uneasy, inept, embarrassed. He felt every inch of her lying upon him; his hands lifted from her shoulders and began to awkwardly pat her on the back. "Don't do that," he pleaded uselessly, feeling her tears soaking into his shirt. "I don't need this kind of aggravation. I knew you'd be trouble." He caught her words. "Awful? What was awful? You could at least look at me." He put a hand under her chin, tilting it up. God! But that was a mistake. She was all sorrowful dark eyes, tear-moist and glistening with an animal innocence. If her tears didn't drown him, those liquid eyes would. "Couldn't you please stop crying."

"I'm trying, *m'sieu.*" She buried her face in his collar, inhaling the erotic smell of him.

"Good...good. Patch. Do you have another name besides Patch?"

"Angelicque Marie Yvette Vidrina Chauvin," she said, sniffling.

Cooper blinked, trying to disregard the slight fluttering of her lips against his neck. "You'll have to tell me how that string of names translates to Patch."

"It doesn't. Papa started it when I was a baby. *Maman* was forever patching me up because I was so clumsy."

"I'm prepared to believe that," Cooper muttered, feeling the damp ground-cold reaching his back.

"What, *m'sieu*?"

"Nothing, just thinking aloud. Now, what was so awful?"

The circle of Cooper's powerful arms was comforting, a magnetic force of protection. She hadn't been hugged in she didn't know how long. She pressed closer, and if there was any doubt in Cooper's mind that she was all woman, it disappeared entirely. Her pulse was a palpable throb in her neck. "Did I hurt you?" she asked.

"Hurt me? I'm as strong as an ox. A little tackle like that is nothing." He thought about getting up, moving her away from him. Just a brief thought. He stopped patting her back and tried to figure out what to do with his hands. "What made you go off your rocker like that?"

"I was seeing Rosalina...seeing it happen all over again." Then she told him about the accident.

"Rosalina is delicate. Mama would never let her help papa. But after he drowned, I had to have help out here, and Rosalina wanted to come. We had our wedding days set, the banns read. Rosalina to marry Gaston, and I was pledged to...oh, it doesn't matter...."

Cooper was digesting this tale, thinking that no woman could be more delicate, more fragile than the one he was soothing now. He suffered a twinge of jealousy aimed at the unnamed suitor. "It wasn't your fault. It sounds to me that your sister was careless, and perhaps she'll be home soon. Only one more operation and she'll be right as rain." He was trying to ignore the delicious excitement building in his loins and was failing miserably.

"I hope so," said Patch, her voice betraying her desperation.

Cooper pulled himself to his feet, bringing her with him. He bent his head, planting a soothing kiss on her forehead. She smelled of soap on fresh skin and an indefinable fragrance he associated with the sun, the wind. He felt a wave of apprehension, but he couldn't stop himself. His arms went around her, his hands sliding down her spine. His voice was barely louder than his pounding heart when he called her name.

A lightness of spirit danced through Patch. Her eyes were a glossy black as she tilted her chin up. Titillating sexual currents were surging strongly between them, making her head reel. "Do you want to kiss me, *m'sieu*?"

"I believe I do," he said hoarsely. Their mouths

came together, his tongue slid over her lips and hers darted out to meet it.

A moan of pleasure broke from deep in Cooper's chest. "I want more than a kiss," he said, pressing his thighs to hers so that there was no doubt to his meaning.

There was something wrong with the timbre of his voice. He was shaky, as excited as she was, Patch realized with awe. He pulled his lips from hers, looking into her eyes, her provocative mouth, waiting . . . .

She was struck by the raw emotion glazing his blue eyes, the boldness of them as they watched her, the seductive creases at the side of his mouth. She was aware of the fire crackling near them, the winter wind ruffling his blond hair, a pair of blue herons soaring on an updraft. And above all she was aware of that part of him that had ignited and was pushing urgently against the soft swell of her belly. She turned away, breathless, dimly realizing that quite against one's will a kiss could lead to something else.

Her heart, body, soul gave a great leap. The impossible was happening. She had no desire to hold back, to resist him. There was simply no way she could deny that to herself. The feeling in the pit of her stomach said it was right. She bet by now all those old fluttering spiderwebs had sizzled up in flames. "We know so little about each other." Reluctant words, but she felt she must speak them.

His fingers bit into her shoulder. "We'll learn. This isn't something that can be put off."

Of course it isn't. "There's so much work—"

"I'll help you later. . . ."

She fought—not too hard—the warmth that weakened her voice, her legs, and lost. She could only nod. Then she was in his arms and being carried inside the camp; he kicked the door closed with his foot.

5

IN THE SILENCE OF THE CAMP Patch allowed Cooper to undress her. She was risking a lot, but she could not have forgone sex with him if all the saints in heaven and the devils in hell had set to clashing right outside the window. His fingers were nimble, his expression intense.... Off came her shirt, her pants, the top half of her insulated underwear—the bottoms. With short breath and fluttering pulse she waited for Cooper to shed his own clothes. He was throwing them every which way, pulling off garments that might have been afire. He was commandingly erect, and she stared unashamedly. She couldn't speak of it, but she knew that she would never envy Una LaBlanc again.

She had lied to Cooper when she told him she had seen naked men before—not a big lie, just a smidgen of one, not even big enough to mention in confession. The closest she had come to seeing a man in his all together was on her twenty-first birthday, when she had lost her virginity to Arlis Lafargue. She had hoped that he would take her dancing at Red's Levee Bar, to celebrate and mingle with her friends. Instead he had driven down the old levee road in his dilapidated truck and parked. Their breaths had misted the windshield, and the night had been so cold they hadn't disrobed. She'd never got an actual glimpse of anything, it being so cold she couldn't concentrate on his nubbin creeping between her thighs for the chilblains sprouting everywhere else. The event had been thoroughly disappointing, and afterward she'd refused intimacy with Arlis, insisting they wait until their marriage bed, where the *act* could be accomplished properly. That was prob'ly what made him go chasing after Una, she thought with reluctant clarity.

Una was welcome to Arlis's domineering swagger, for she could see that Cooper was the stuff with which she could be certain of children, grandchildren and happiness. For an instant she let her mind move rapidly forward, imagining her family made. Then Cooper was beside her in the bed, the length of him pressing against her, and she felt his nakedness on her everywhere.

The future receded, becoming present as his hands explored her flesh, his fingers stroking the sides of her breasts, making the muscles go taut, the nipples deeply pink and erect.

She uttered small garbled words of pleasure, managing only, "This is a good omen, no?" as she delivered herself fully into his hands, wanting to make him need her forever.

Cooper was trying to comprehend the meaning of the omen, but his mind wouldn't accept anything beyond love talk. "You're wonderful," he breathed. "Skin like velvet...so soft...so pliable." Their coming together was easy and natural. He felt her silken length against him, back, legs, the warmth of her breasts on his flesh. Her lavender-soap scent enveloped him.

Patch was thrilled, glorying in his words because he wasn't complaining her small breasts. She arched her back so that they were uplifted and displayed for his lips, offering them wantonly. She could feel the need for him rising in her...growing to bursting, a pressure that made it difficult for her to breathe. All of her opened to meet him, to welcome him as his throbbing body strained with reckless elation. She moved over him, lifting her hips to his so that Cooper was driven to grasp her, pulling her forward as he straightened his legs and lay out full length with Patch impaled, enclosing him in her shimmering flesh. His compelling eyes seemed to burn into her soul, and she felt exposed beyond her nakedness. But then the sensations....

He drew her head to his, her lips to his, taking succor there, thrusting his tongue deep into her mouth.

She swayed above him as his lips suckled, his tongue caressed, and every nerve in her was seized with craving for him, so that she moved to his rhythm hoarsely moaning Cajun words of love.

"I want to do everything with you," said Cooper, and he did. The pleasure he gave her was as precious to him as the pleasure he took, so that Patch became a kind of extension of his being, yet with a being of her own that had to be respected.

"And I with you," she answered, letting her hands and lips run over his hard body with joyous fervor.

She kept her eyes open in sensual ecstasy, wanting to see as well as feel the expressions changing on Cooper's face, the way his hands and lips created this new magic within her. She was thinking, *I'm seeing this...I'm feeling this*, and it touched her profoundly. His body vibrated with a powerful tension and she succumbed to bliss.

The explosion of release stunned her, making her fall forward, collapsing upon his strong chest as she called his name from a faraway place. It seemed to drive Cooper into a frenzy. He rolled her onto her back, his lips devouring hers, his tongue a demon as he mounted her and took her superbly. Patch realized that what she had had with Arlis Lafargue was like dust on the wind. A knowing passed through her, and she metamorphosed from girl into woman. Oh, now she understood why *maman* had changed so since papa had died, and why *grand-mère* longed for the return of *grand-père*.

Cooper's breath was in her ear, telling her she was lovely. A fierce and secret fire began to burn at her very core. She drew her hands down his back, feeling the rough ridges of his muscles like uncarved granite. Then his lips parted with a shuddering gasp and he was still. Patch made a little whimpering noise at the emptiness in her as he pulled away and lay at her side.

She moved her head to his shoulder, nestling inside the circle of his arm as she tugged the blanket over their nakedness. For a little while, as they caught their breath, neither moved.

It's right what we did, Patch thought, turning on her side to look at Cooper, her own man. How could she ever have thought this was the road to perdition? *Grand-mère* was right, fate was the province of God. She saw Cooper's strong brow, his blunt blond lashes, his sharp blue eyes, his straight nose—not so straight looking from the side. His handsome manliness pierced her heart. Nothing bad could come out of what they'd done. It was a hundred times lovelier than she'd expected—and she wanted to do it again. She mentioned it shyly and Cooper croaked, "No, not yet."

But when Patch thought something she just sort of stuck to it. Her narrow little hands went exploring, beginning again, taking him with her. "Can you feel this? This?" and before long Cooper acquiesced; he had no choice and didn't want one.

Afterward the pure sensation of rightness soared still higher in Patch. She was consumed with elation. She and Cooper were bound together for al-

ways, the same as if their banns had been announced in church. "I feel like we ought to do something else," she told him.

Thinking she meant more sex, his answer was
weak, immediate. "You're depraved," he whispered.

Patch gave an arch smile. "I only meant we ought
to shake hands or something, no? Yes—that's it,
we'll shake on it." She took his great paw in hers
and pumped vigorously, using her own strength;
Cooper was limp.

She regarded him and smiled. "We will tell each
other our secrets," she whispered, going first. "I've
never given myself to a man so completely."

Weakly he raised up on his elbow, looking down
at her, letting his fingers get lazily lost in her cap of
dark brown curls. "You do this often with other
men?" His tone was flat.

Patch felt a chill, and some warning consciousness
spoke to her of the value of discretion. "No. I was en-
gaged once," she told him, as if that explained it all.

Cooper expelled a sigh and fell back, accepting reality, not liking it and wondering who the man had
been. His male ego felt a pang. "I shouldn't have
asked. It's none of my business what you do, or with
whom."

Patch stared at him for a paralyzed moment.
There was something in his tone, something that
baffled her, something that she ought to understand.
When it came to her she felt kissed and damned by
fate. Her hands flew to her ears, as if she could stop
his words from entering her brain. "*M'sieu*, you
can't mean what you say! This is only the beginning."

Cooper felt a hobbling panic. "Now wait a minute! You're trying to pull a farmer's daughter act on
me. Forget it."

"Farmer's daughter? What farmer's daughter?"

she asked, shaking, and Cooper took the measure of her worldliness. Patch scrambled to her knees, forgetful of her nakedness, speaking volumes with her hands in her bewilderment. She knew him intimately now. His eyes were bluer, deeper, his skin more fine, his shoulders wider. And his chest with all its wonderful golden hair was so near. Yet she couldn't touch it, couldn't run her fingers through it because of the barrier he'd thrown up between them. "You gave yourself to me, Cooper," she said gravely, using his name for the first time. Her words sounded like a melody. "I gave myself to you—"

"It was something we both wanted. I'm not the staying kind. The way you're carrying on you'd have me marching down the aisle in fifteen minutes. I warned you, I don't get involved."

She half perceived, watching him, that he had no inner clarity. That once he had made up his mind he was a certain way, you could hang the difference on the end of his nose and he wouldn't see it.

"Makin' love *is* getting involved," she said in a desperate little voice.

"I call it out and out lust."

Her eyes narrowed to slits, studying his face. It was a mask, and his eyes were hard as stone.

A twinge of conscience, having mostly to do with her innocence, made Cooper put his hand gently on her arm. Her whole being was quivering, her little breasts with their saucy nipples thrusting toward him in her dismay just as they had in love. He wanted her all over again. "Why don't you put on some clothes?" he suggested, beginning to edge off the bed.

Patch didn't want to be gentled. "You don't want to understand. You belong to me. God gave you to me." Her utter logic bypassed Cooper like a misdirected arrow.

"God gave me to you?" He was incredulous. "Wrapped me up and put me under your tree like a puppy dog, I suppose?"

She closed her eyes and threw her head back in exasperation. It was no use.

Cooper watched her lovely neck grow taut, the hollows deepen. He discovered his mouth was suddenly dry. He had been more open, more candid with Patch than with any other woman. "Listen," he said gutturally, "we had sex together, that's all. It wasn't something that was fated by the gods."

He backed off the bed, keeping her in his sight as he began picking his clothes up from the floor. The expression he wore closed her out, veiling an inner sanctum she was not allowed to penetrate. "You're scared," she said in a voice barely audible, but with a recognition that went bone deep.

He couldn't make sense of what she was saying. "You're crazy. Nothing scares me."

"You're afraid of falling in love. You're afraid of me."

He had his shirt and pants on now, yet for a moment he had an odd sense of existing outside of time. "You're making a mountain out of a molehill," he retorted, but he was looking at her in a strange way.

"No, I'm not. I watched you, watched your face when you were making love to me. There was something wondrous in your expression, as if you'd never made love quite that intensely before, no?"

"I just found you unfailingly refreshing, that's all."

"You see," she went on feelingly, as though he hadn't spoken, "I asked God for a patient man—"

A glimmer of understanding flitted through his muddled brain. "Your guy hasn't shown up yet. I'm impatient, stubborn...even mean. You jumped to the wrong conclusion when you met me. And this is the stupidest conversation I've ever had. God giving me as a gift. That's a twist.''

"You're probably the best God could do on such short notice," she replied with utter belief and simplicity. "I'm not giving you back." She'd just have to wait until he felt it way down in the pit of his stomach, aching there until it wouldn't let go.

He looked at her helplessly. Patch got off the bed and glided serenely and wholly naked to the stove, putting water to boil for bathing. She had a lovely back, a fetching posterior over which his hands had fit perfectly. The steel in his paradoxical character began to melt and puddle at his feet. "Aren't you cold?" he asked.

"No, *m'sieu*, I'm used to it."

He had to save himself. He grabbed up his duffel and began shoving his things into it, the testing kit with all its vials, the charts, spare clothes. "I think the best thing all around is for me to leave."

Patch bent over to put the big tin dishpan on the floor, then stepped into it. Seeing her, Cooper moaned and dragged a hand over his face.

"Did you hear me? I said I'm leaving."

Patch was lathering up. She stopped and looked at him. "I heard you."

He packed, she bathed.

Cooper dragged his duffel to the door, leaning it against the wall, then looked out the window. "There's just enough daylight left to get us into Catahoula."

"I have to run my traps, and I won't be going in until I've turned five hundred pelts. Rosalina needs the money for her operation."

His eyes went cold, like the hard blue ice of a glacier. "What are you implying? You can't keep me prisoner here. I'll hitch a ride with the first trapper I see headed back to civilization."

"You do that, *m'sieu*, but our fates are settled." She glared at him for a moment. "And if you're a prisoner it's of your own making. I only said a prayer. I didn't send you a written invitation."

She then turned her lovely backside to him, picked up a pitcher of warm water and poured it over herself, rinsing off the soap. That done, she took the old flannel sheet that served for a towel, dried herself thoroughly, then wrapped it about her as she moved gracefully about the camp gathering her clothes. She knew Cooper was watching her out the corner of his eye, and she knew, too, the effect she was having on him. It wasn't that she wanted him to suffer, but she'd use whatever powers and wiles were available to her to make him see that they belonged together. The vexation lay in the waiting....

"Fates!" he reiterated snidely. "You sound like a Gypsy fortune teller." He waited for a response, but Patch had hit on one of the most useful weapons a woman can employ—silence. She dipped into the small trunk that held her personables, retrieved a bottle of baby lotion and began to massage it into her face, hands and elbows.

Leaning now on the back of one of the rickety chairs, Cooper scowled. "Don't you have anything to say about that?"

Patch dabbed lotion on her knees.

"Well, I have. As long as I'm here, I'll have to work. I can't go around wasting the government's money."

Patch sniffed, more eloquent than any words she could have chosen to let him know what she thought. She screwed the lid back on the lotion, stored it away, brushed her hair without benefit of a mirror, then began stepping into her clothes piece by piece.

He scowled at her. "I know what you're thinking.

A nine-year-old can fill little bottles with mud and water samples."

Feeling a reply flying to her tongue, Patch bit her lips to hold it back.

Cooper was getting riled. "I don't like sulking women, they're anathema to me." He ferreted around in his duffel, brought out his charts and kit and slammed them on the table. "This is important work, even if you don't approve. You agreed to act as guide, remember?"

She sat on the floor to lace her boots.

"The sooner I get the survey done, the quicker I can get back to Washington." He caught Patch sneaking a look at him from beneath her thick lashes. He feigned a sigh. "You ought to see my apartment. Only three rooms, but I built floor-to-ceiling shelves to display my wood sculptures. I have a built-in stereo and a large collection of records. My landlady loves to come up to listen. I can't wait to get home." He closed his eyes, pretending to ruminate, and a moment later was rewarded by the slam of the camp door as Patch stomped out.

He clenched his fists in a frustration scoured with confusion. He couldn't believe Patch really wanted him—he wouldn't believe it. A childhood of being unwanted was not easily forgotten. "She's making me out to be a fool," he said to the empty room.

Patch did not think Cooper a fool, just stubborn and filled with all the wrong notions. She contemplated his threat to leave. She could prevent that. She knew the habits of every trapper in the basin; none would be going into town until they had a real mess of pelts to sell. Except Arlis. If he ran out of beer, or coffee, or cigarettes, he'd make the daylong trip—unless he could save himself the trouble by borrowing. Much as it galled her, she'd save him those trips if the need arose.

She glanced up at the shack to see Cooper jerk back from the window. *Starting to feel it already,* she thought in a wave of emotion. Turning her back, she set to dipping traps in the warm peanut oil.

When she finished oiling traps it was almost dark, and in the winter cold she was blowing white plumes of visible breath. But another task nagged at her, so she wrangled the skiff into the shallow canal back of the camp, fueled its small motor and left to set out the fish trap in a deep fast-moving stream.

Cooper heard the motor and stepped out onto the narrow deck that served as a back porch. He yelled. Patch turned, a dark shadow in the melting night, and lifted her hand in a snappy wave. Waving wasn't talking, she thought, and switching on the boat lamp to guide her way, felt the exhilaration she did every season first time on the water.

He watched her until she disappeared behind the gaudy yellowing swamp grass that seemed unwilling to give up its color to night shadows. He didn't know why, but he felt a sharp stab of fear for her. She looked so tiny out there by herself, and when the swamp swallowed her up, he gave a foolish thought to not being in such a hurry to get her out of his life.

THE WIND BLEW HARD out of the north as if it was in a hurry to reach the temperate climate of the warm Gulf seas. Patch nestled her rounded chin behind the grating roughness of her collar and kept a sharp lookout.

It took her an hour to find just the right spot to set the fish hoop. Afterward, with the lamp on the boat aided by a weak moon splattering golden light, she wandered the labyrinth of shallow canals, looking for trap sites for nutria and muskrat. The muskrat were plentiful this year. She had come upon hun-

dreds and hundreds of their grassy dens. She was
buoyant with the sense that everything good comes
to those who wait. She had her man, at least his
presence; trapping promised to be good and that
meant money for Rosalina's operation. And after
that, Rosalina would be coming home. Patch believed it. She had to believe it.

She was pleasantly exhausted by the time she tied
the skiff to the rusted iron ring in the bulwark that
kept the drying sheds from sliding into the canal.
Her ear caught the steady throbbing of the generator. So Cooper had figured out how to get the electricity going. She came out from behind the shed,
her boots noiseless on the soft earth, and stood for a
minute gazing at the lighted windows. There was a
steady warmth in her as she remembered their elec-
trifying coupling. Prob'ly he'd been mulling on it
the whole time she'd been gone. The thought made
gooseflesh erupt along her arms and legs, and she
closed her eyes to let the erotic pictures grow more
real. She felt once again how her bones had seemed
to lose all substance in that last climactic moment. A
sigh escaped, the wind snatched it away, and she decided to wait until morning to speak to Cooper, for
he spouted more about himself to her silence than he
had to all her probing questions. Landladies and
farmer's daughters! He would soon forget all about
them.

She burst into the camp with her cheeks rosy and
her eyes dancing. Cooper looked up at her warily,
but Gaston Voisin, who was sitting across from him,
rose from his chair and came over to slap Patch on
the back in greeting.

"Didn't expect me, no?" teased Gaston, grinning.
Gaston was younger than she by two years and
pledged to Rosalina. He had an olive complexion, a
sensitive melancholy face with great dark eyes and a

thatch of unruly black hair. He was devoted to her
sister.

"No, where's your boat?"

"My brother, he's bringing it tomorrow. I hitched
a ride out with Indian Jack's partner. Thought I
could buy me a bed with you tonight...." He threw
out a lean work-worn hand to indicate the wooden
sink counter where a pile of fish lay.

Patch smiled. "That'll buy you a layabout on the
sofa. I see you've met Cooper," she added casually,
careful not to look Cooper's way as she removed her
hat, gloves and jacket. But her sharp eye had not
missed the pile of cigarette butts accumulated in the
can at his elbow, testimony to his worrying over her,
she imagined.

"He's been telling me about his work."

Patch wrinkled her nose.

"He doesn't really like it," she lied.

"He's been telling me that, too," said Gaston.
"We'll just have to make a Cajun out of him, no?"

Her breath quickened. "I'd better fry those fish."
This she did, knowing that every chance he got,
Cooper was looking at her. The fluttery restlessness
in her stomach left little room for food, but neither
man noticed that she only picked at her meal. Relax-
ing afterward, Cooper and Gaston smoked cigarettes.

Wanting Patch to talk to him but not wanting her
to know it, Cooper said, "I've a bottle of Jack Daniels
in my duffel. Anybody want a drink?"

"Lor, yes!" said Gaston. Cooper waited for a response from Patch. He could feel the tension humming in the air between them, yet Gaston appeared
oblivious to it.

She cast him a haughty sidelong glance, picked a
spot on the wall and announced to no one in particular, "I'd better get going on the dishes."

After she had done them, she opened the door and stood there as she did every night breathing in the cold air, but enjoying the warmth from the stove on her back. She seemed to have no control over herself—her nipples were rigid, her body going all moist by itself. She couldn't seem to stop it even though she chased all thought of Cooper from her conscious mind. Her body just kept right on remembering him.

Cooper was laughing at some joke Gaston had told, and when his laughter died they were unusually silent for a time. She heard Gaston clear his throat. He was oft times shy and his rough, older brothers delighted in making him blush. "Say, Patch," he called softly. "Any word from Rosalina?"

Now she understood what had brought him to her camp. She turned her head slightly so that her voice would carry to him. "Another operation...."

"Another?"

She winced at the pain in his voice.

"Have you had a letter? She mentioned me, no?"

"No letter. *Maman* talked to the doctor."

His heaving sigh filled the small room. "I'm going to see her this Christmas. Never mind she says not to come. This Christmas I'm going. It's been a year."

There was utter longing in his voice. Patch recognized it for what it was because she was experiencing it herself for Cooper. For a fleeting moment she wondered if Rosalina and Gaston had made love. She hoped so, but it made her guilt over Rosalina's accident more poignant. In Rosalina's first letter home, written in the scrawling hand of a hospital aide, she had begged their promise not to come see her. Begged them to wait until she was beautiful once again. She and Gaston had given their word, never dreaming Rosalina would be gone a year. Only *maman* went to see her, once a month, taking

the bus to Baton Rouge. "She'll be mad at you for
going back on your word, Gaston."

"So? What's mad, no? What do I care about a little
skin on the face, a lopsided ear? We're pledged to
each other. I'll talk her out of that place," he added
fervently. The whiskey bottle clinked against glass,
and Patch knew he was pouring himself another
drink.

"Time for lights out," she said, closing the door.

"I'll do it," Cooper volunteered. He put on his
jacket, picked up the flashlight and went outside to
switch off the generator.

A few minutes later the only sounds were the rustling of the three of them as they disrobed in the
dark. Patch was tired, her body yearning for sleep.
But her thoughts, all having to do with Cooper, who
was tossing and turning in his bunk across the
room, kept her awake. She turned over, hugging a
pillow to her bosom, but it was a sad replacement
for Cooper's strong body. If Gaston had not been
bunked down on the sofa between them, she would
have swiftly traded the pillow for the real thing,
pride be damned. Without saying a word, prob'ly,
acknowledging that her body would be speaking a
language all its own.

Cooper was afire with visions of saucy nipples
and a fetching posterier. He could feel the contours
of her body, and the smell of freshness of her hair. A
certain part of him was so tumescent with desire he
was thinking the only way to rid himself of the
agony was to offer the damn thing a pair of pajamas
and the other half of his bunk.

6

PATCH SET THE TABLE for breakfast, adding a bowl of apples and oranges, using the action to cast a surreptitious glance Cooper's way. With an elbow crooked over his eyes he was lying in his bunk, pretending to be asleep yet managing to appear more sour than a jar of clabbered cream. Her not talking to him was adding fuel to his acrimony. Suddenly her conscience burned in an acutely painful manner wholly new to her. Why, she was feeling bad for making him miserable.

The early-morning wind mewed by, catching in odd nooks and crannies. Moss swayed with royal dignity; a gull flew past the window, stark white, beating against the wind. Loose bits of tar paper flapped rhythmically, *tat-tat-tatter-tat*, like a song needing words. Patch lifted her head listening, making up words, *Go to Cooper—go! Go to Cooper—go!* She closed her eyes, breathing quietly, letting a sense of magnanimity grow within her. It gave her a warm sense of comfort and strength, and in her mind she heard him calling her. Her skin tingled, woefully hot. Well, she couldn't stay cross with him forever. She padded over to him, sidestepping the sofa where Gaston snored gently, and sat on the edge of the bunk.

"How're you feeling today, Cooper?"

Moving his elbow, he eyed her loftily. "Do I dare believe my ears? The swamp goddess has come down from her perch in a willow tree and found her tongue? Why the sudden interest in my health?"

Swamp goddess! She didn't pick up the derision in his voice. She was radiantly, shamefully happy. Her heart swelled with love. "I'm going to be nice to you, Cooper. I've forgiven you for those mean things you said yesterday." She lowered her voice. "I thought perhaps you were worn out because of what we did."

He dropped her a mocking, down-turned smile. "My little friend," he said softly, "I can do that every day and twice on Sunday."

She drew her fingertips lightly over the quilt, underneath which was one of his legs. "I don't think so—you tried to beg off that second time. But no matter, we won't have time to do it every day."

Cooper caught his breath. "Get off my bed," he choked. "Get off my bed."

She looked at him obliquely, while her hand, minding its own will, crept along his leg. "It's funny. I can't stop thinking about sex, and I used never to even give it a thought—except to say no."

He caught her hand as it came to the juncture of his thighs, but not before she felt the rising there. "Cut that out!" he ordered.

"I just wanted to touch you," she said with a satisfied little smile tugging sharply at her lips. He was hers. Oh, how completely he was hers.

His face darkened. He wouldn't give in, not in a million years, not after that snide remark. A tart, that's all she was, talking out about a man's prowess like that. A tart. He knew a lot about tarts—he'd been born to one. "You just want to start something you can't finish." He angled a silent nod at Gaston. "Now get off my bunk so I can get up."

She gave him a provocative smile. "We've made up our first real fight, now, yes?"

He had a sick falling sensation in his stomach. "You're crazy," he whispered.

Her smile lifted to the fathomless depths of her
dark eyes. "No one's ever called me a swamp goddess. You say such pretty things. I like that almost as
much as making love."

"It's useless, what you're thinking," he said, clinging to his stubbornness with the pertinacity of melted
gum on hot pavement.

"No, it isn't. God's on our side. I doubted it some,
but now I know."

When food was ready and coffee poured, Patch
woke Gaston.

"A good breakfast gets a man off to a fine start, eh,
Cooper?" he said when he joined them at the table.
"Our Patch can sure cook, no?"

"Food is food," said Cooper, striking a covert
glance at the woman sitting across from him. He had
planned to be as stingy in his conversation today as
she had been yesterday, but he guessed with Gaston
at the table, that would be impossible.

After the men had finished, lighted up cigarettes,
inhaled deeply and emitted gusty sighs of satisfaction, Patch stacked dishes in the sink, then prepared
to go outdoors.

"You have work I can help you with until my
brother arrives?" Gaston asked.

"No. You keep Cooper company awhile. I'm only
sorting mold boards for pelts this morning, then later I have to take Cooper to do some of his tests...
along that old soil heap where the oil company cut a
canal."

Cooper came alert. "I don't work on Saturdays or
Sundays."

Gaston's jaw dropped. "No?"

"You'll work this Saturday," Patch said witheringly. "And, Sunday, too." She whisked Cooper's
cup and saucer from the table, tossing them into the
tin dishpan, the clatter a display of her displeasure.

"Government hours don't hold in the swamp. Here we work with nature in season and out, not against it." He had so much to learn, she thought despairingly.

Cooper's eyes narrowed until they were knifelike slits in his ruddy, unshaven face. Before he could form a reply Gaston leaned forward eagerly, helpfully. "You must learn our customs, our habits, *m'sieu*," he said, and then added slyly, "Also our women. Spoiled rotten they are, just like that soil bank you must inspect today."

Patch was gazing out the window toward the shed; she didn't flick an eyelid. "I'll have the boat ready to go in two hours." She tapped the old windup clock on the stove, emphasizing her words, and smiled sweetly at Cooper as she made her exit.

Gaston was laughing. "Ah, *m'sieu*, Patch has put her name on you. If you want out of it, you will have to buy a gris-gris from the old crone who lives with Indian Jack."

"A gris-gris?" Cooper inquired, and then wished he hadn't.

"A potion to protect your heart," Gaston informed him.

Cooper dragged a hand over his face, feeling beard stubble. Prayers, a gris-gris, a swamp goddess who insisted he was a gift from heaven—it was too much for a man like himself. "When are you going back to town, Gaston? May I have a lift?"

"But of course, *m'sieu*. Christmas Eve. My brother and I will pick you up."

Cooper's heart sank. "That's almost four weeks from now. I imagine Patch will be going in before that." He moved from the table to heat water for shaving.

Gaston watched him with a baleful eye. "You should have your woman do that for you," he said.

Cooper smarted. "I don't have a woman, but if I did, I wouldn't ask her to do beans."

Gaston sighed with Gallic insight, offering sympathy. "Falling in love is hard on a man, no? I'm happy to be beyond the point with Rosalina that you're suffering now with Patch."

Cooper turned from the tiny shaving mirror hanging lopsided on the wall and stared at Gaston with horror-stricken eyes. "I'm not in love. I don't believe in love."

Gaston looked superior in his pity. "There's an iron quality in a Cajun woman that no others possess, *m'sieu*. They're courtesans, Patch and Rosalina more than most. Did you know they're descendants of the casket girls brought to New Orleans to become wives of those men who built that city up from the swamps? Old Grand-mère Duval, she still has the tiny trunk her great, great, great, and perhaps another great *grand-mère* brought with her on the ship. If Patch wants you...." He spread his hands in an expressive gesture.

Cooper turned back to the mirror feeling like he was caught in quicksand. The more he tried to extricate himself, the deeper he sank. He didn't like having it put into words as succinctly as Gaston had. The silence he had planned to bestow on Patch he now directed at the young man.

He began to think of Patch as brazenly unconventional, ruthless in trying to attract him, snare him. Her kind ran loose all over Washington. He had protected himself there with ease; he could do it here. And the sooner he finished his work, the quicker he'd be back in civilization where women didn't go around saying indolently that his presence was a gift from God, then making flip remarks about the way things were done in bed. He was too intelligent to fall for her kind of sorcery.

IT WAS COLD, the air a heavy moist substance you could touch but scarcely breathe. Away from the protected bulwarks of the camp the wind whipped mercilessly, undulating the swamp grass until it lay limp in mud. It broke over the two occupants in the small flat-bottomed boat, making them hunch down inside their coats.

The skiff had thwarts at prow and stern, but no seat at midship where its small diesel-powered motor was bolted to the decking. A hand-held piece of flexible, twisted wire running from in front of the motor to holes drilled beneath the back thwart was a simple rudder guide. In front of the motor Patch and Cooper knelt, propping their buttocks on the heels of their boots for comfort.

Cooper was continuing his introspection about Patch. He told himself she was just a bit of fluff. Her cheeks were too red, her curls too slick and her eyelashes too long. Her lilting accent was a trick of his ears, what with the absence of city smells, noises, flashing traffic and crowds to dilute it. He had it together now...as long as he didn't think about her curious naked dignity as she'd bathed in the tin dishpan or the way her hand had traveled up his thigh that morning.

Patch saw a range of expressions pass over Cooper's features. She noted that giveaway tilt of mocking scorn at the edge of his mouth that states an internal masculine ego has warred and won, and recognized the gloating as the same as Arlis's after he'd bedded Una. She twisted the tiller cable around her little finger, uttering a painful flutelike, "Ohhhh."

"What's happened?" Cooper snapped from his reverie, speaking above the whine of the engine.

"It's nothing," she said with deliberate carelessness. "I just caught my finger."

"You don't have to act so brave about it," he replied. "Let me see." He pulled off her cotton work glove, inspecting her fingers, which were reddened by the cold. "At least the skin's not broken. Put your glove on, and let me take the tiller. I can't get us into too much trouble as narrow as these canals are."

"You're sure, yes?"

"Of course, I'm sure." He traded places with her and never felt the mythical quicksand reach his knees.

Patch wound the red muffler Grand-mère Duval had knitted about the lower part of her face. It kept her warm and hid her smile while her heart pounded stupidly.

HE WORKED THE SOIL BANK, taking his samples, while Patch kept an unobtrusive eye on him, leading him around safe-looking but treacherous bog, logs with loose bark where sleeping snakes, easily riled, were hidden. Hurrying him past an area where there were fresh wolf droppings. When they returned to the small boat, she muffled the sound as she clicked the safety catch on her rifle.

"Think I'll sit on the thwart for a while," Cooper said. "My knees were getting sore."

"Mine sting some, too," Patch declared. "Started yesterday from straddling you."

Oh, good creeping damn! "Nice girls don't talk that way."

Patch's hands stilled on the throttle, heart pounding in her throat. Her mouth was dry, swallowing hurt as she might with a very sore throat. "They don't? What do they talk about?"

"Clothes, children, cooking, things like that."

"Oh." She didn't have much in the way of clothes, no children at all—yet. Cooking? *Grand-mère* had filled her in on recipes and made her swear not to give them out. She sighed and brightened. "I'm going to show you where I killed my first snake."

She took him on a tour of her childhood. "See that spit of land about a yard wide? Papa put me off to pick blackberries while he went to set out crawfish traps. That's where I killed it, and it acting like it was a stick. I shot its head straight off with my .22. I was ten years old."

As they entered a wide pond deep in the bayou surrounded by scrub oak dripping gray lace, Patch said, "Biggest catfish you ever did see in this pond, but you can't catch 'em. You don't dare drop a hook else an alligator'll swallow it and let you reel him in as pretty as you please, swimming along so you don't feel the weight until, snap! He takes your hand or leg or whatever. See that little bit of wharf? That's where I took my first alligator. You use a big hook on a strong rope and dangle the bait above the water. Soon's your partner pulls it in you shoot it right between the eyes."

"Lots of alligators around here?" asked Cooper through cold-stiffened lips.

"Hundreds of them, all sleeping in the mud. We're sailing right over them."

"How deep is this pond?"

"Not deep at all. 'Bout four feet, five along the middle, but you can't see too much from there."

Cooper shifted to the middle of the thwart.

"Alligator tail is succulent, better than pork. *Grand-mère* has some in the freezer. I'll bring a roast back with us next time." That was talking about cooking, she thought. Cooper'd be pleased. She looked expectantly at him over her shoulder.

"That'd be nice," he muttered, turning slightly to observe their wake, wondering if it was stirring any monsters from their rest.

"See that willow brake? I saw a bear in there last year. Used to be a rare sight to see a bear, but they're coming back. Refuge department will let us have a season on them one year soon, I imagine."

"Bears hibernate in the winter."

"They do mostly, guess it's a good thing. Coyotes and wild hogs winter in that brake now."

"Steer to the middle, why don't you?"

"I told you, you can't see anything from there. Besides, the willows cut the wind. It'd be colder out there. Another thing, opposite side of the brake is a bit of bad water. You might want to take samples."

Cooper wished strongly he was doing something safe—like following a toxic-chemical dump truck that had a bully riding shotgun. "Next time we're out this way," he said.

"Might not get this way again, though. Prob'ly not, trapping season starts tomorrow."

"I don't have any empty sample bottles left."

"Oh, too bad, no?" She smiled at him proudly. "You worked too hard at that other soil bank."

First piece of luck he'd had all week, thought Cooper, and the returning smile he gave Patch was genuine.

The sky looked frostbitten, going gray with dusk hard upon the swamp. "I know you're enjoying this, and I hate to cut it short," said Patch, "but we have to be turning toward camp. It's getting dark, and there's still supper to be cooked, dishes and all."

"I don't mind a bit."

Patch swung the boat eastward with a tremor of expectancy running through her body.

The camp smelled of garlic and onions and melting cheese, making Cooper's stomach growl with hunger. He washed his hands in soapy bayou water that Patch had heated, dried them on a rag that hung from a pair of antlers, then leaned over her shoulder to see what was cooking. Another hunger began to grow, one that went bone deep and that no earthly food could satisfy. He spun away from her, cursing his lack of control.

Water and mud samples that he had collected, along with his charts, were scattered on the table, waiting to be properly labeled, recorded and stored away. He set to work, but his concentration was ragged.

Patch sensed his unease and her anticipation grew. He was wanting her. She heard his pencils scratching on paper, heard the points snap time and again, listened for his muttered expletives. "Better clear the table, Cooper, supper's almost ready," she said at last.

The day spent out-of-doors had made them ravenous, and the first few minutes at the table were spent eating. Sounds in the shack of coffee simmering, forks scraping plates, sighs of satisfaction mingled with those more distant—the faint slapping of water against the wharf as the tide came in; the murmur of the wind, softened now as it brushed the eaves; the last worrisome chatter of birds settling in nearby willows for the night. Patch set her fork aside, listening, for it was a moment worth savoring. Outside was a world that she moved through freely and confidently. Inside she was plagued with a willful impatience, and there was the added excitement of what was to come. It pushed a question out of her mind onto her tongue. "Cooper, do you think I'm a nice girl?"

The manly self-pity he'd suffered at Patch's hands that morning had faded some, but he answered with caution. "I didn't mean you weren't nice. It's just that I don't usually talk about sex with women, and they don't talk about it with me. And you ought not start talking about it now."

"Maybe other women don't like doing it with you. Prob'ly not. If they did, they'd tell you. Like I do."

He made a little moaning sound.

Patch's eyes suddenly glowed. "Is your stomach aching? Does it feel like you have spiders or anything crawling around in it?"

"The pain is somewhere else." He spoke from low in his throat, like he was coming down with a cold.

Patch eyed him narrowly. Talking of alligator roasts hadn't set things right between them. "I like that gray turtleneck sweater you wear. Think next time I'm to Catahoula, I'll buy me one."

"You do that."

Talk didn't seem to be of much use. Patch sighed and told herself again that he was a man worth having. "Tomorrow we put out traps. If you want to bring your sample bottles, you can."

"I might. I got a week's work done today, though."

"Have you ever done any skinning?" She took up her fork again.

"Helped butcher a hog once."

"Ugh. Too grisly."

"Delivered a calf all by myself when I was eight."

"Not the same. Never mind, I'll teach you."

He grinned, etching the grooves in his face into deep relief. "You really think you can turn me into a trapper in the few weeks I'll be here?"

Turn you into something besides what you are, she thought determinedly. "Don't talk about leaving," she warned. "I'm not sure what you'll turn out to be. You're no bargain, being as you contract yourself out to the government and all, and especially not . . . ." She stopped in midsentence, sensing immediately that the remainder of her comment would be a mistake.

"Especially not what?" he asked, intrigued, while his eyes dropped slowly to examine the rapid rise and fall of her small breasts. If she made any more remarks about bed games, he was in the mood to change her mind.

"You're baiting me, no?"

"Especially not what?" he insisted.

"You have Satyr eyes."

His lids fell. "My eyes are blue."

"It's not the color, it's the message in them."

"Most women tell me I have an irresistible smile and sensitive eyes."

She felt a prick of indignation. "Among these admirers is your beautiful landlady no doubt, and a farmer's daughter or two?"

"No doubt," he said, and bent his attention to the food on his plate.

"What do they know?" she snapped.

Later, feeling generous, Cooper dried and put away dishes while Patch washed. No Cajun man would be so noble, but Patch kept her own counsel. When he was once again bent over his charts and notebook, she sat on her bunk, brushing her hair. His was also wind-ravished, sticking up all over his head, and in the light from the incandescent bulb it looked like flickering gold. She felt the most extraordinary urge to walk across the room and smooth it down.

As if divining her thoughts, his hand went up, his fingers threading his hair. "That's enough for today, considering it's Saturday," he said, standing up to stretch.

"Want to play dominos?"

"No. I think I'm going to have to tackle that dishpan."

"A bath?" Her lilt hid the quaver, but her eyes shone unnaturally bright. She had been thinking of bathing herself, but now felt suddenly shy about him seeing her nude. Being nice had its limitations. She would wait until lights out.

"Yes, a bath with lots of hot water. This mopping at my face and hands with a rag has left me feeling grimy."

"I'll get the water going." She did, and turned on two extra burners to warm the room to ward off gooseflesh.

She sat on the sofa, as stiff as a moldboard while he soaped and sloshed. His feet fit into the pan, but when he poured rinse water over his broad shoulders, not a drop ended up in the pan. "Damn, I hope you have a mop," he called to her.

It took immense effort on her part not to turn her head. "Something wrong, *m'sieu*?"

"I'm making a mess, is all. Where's a towel?"

"Towel?" Patch felt feeble flutterings in her windpipe. The piece of flannel was lying on the box at the foot of her bunk. Knowing his eyes were on her, she lifted a hand and pointed.

"Hand it to me, will you? No sense me dripping water all over the linoleum."

Cooper's face took on a bland expression as she went to retrieve the toweling. "Thanks," he said, when she was standing, facing him. He did not let go of her gaze nor did it waver. She could see suddenly that he was trying just as hard as she was to figure everything out. Then he grasped her wrist, holding her in his space. Droplets of water clung to golden hairs on his chest. "This isn't one of the things I deem needs privacy," he said seductively.

The flannel began to slip between her fingers. "It isn't?" Her lungs were emptying of air and an erotic current shot down her spine. She didn't have any nerves in her body; they were flying out her feet. His arm slid about her, welding her to his hard contours until she felt him rising hard against her soft thighs. As she lifted her face to his, her lips parting in welcome, an understanding dawned about the man he

was. He didn't like talking about sex because he was
a doer. When his mouth hovered far too long she
pressed closer, driven by desire to initiate the kiss,
and her hips of their own accord undulated against
his.

His warm moist tongue thrust gently at first, as
though exploring a thing long savored, but the
touch of her swaying hips put violence in his embrace and a savagery in his tongue. When his lips
came away from hers, his eyes were heavy with desire, his breathing ragged. "Take off your clothes,"
he murmured urgently, setting her apart from him
so that he could retrieve the flannel from the floor.

He turned from her and a soft gasp caught in her
throat. His back was crisscrossed with white welts,
old scars. She had seen those welts through his
shirts, felt them when they were making love, but
had thought they were the ridges of his taut muscles. "Cooper! What happened to your back?"

He spun about, his face swimming in the light
bulb's golden aureole, his mouth drawn into a harsh
line as though he were a golden warrior bent on a
fiendish task. All sexual nuance fell from his voice.
"Nothing."

Patch went very, very cold, involuntarily taking a
backward step. "Yes, it did." Her voice was low, as if
she knew this was perhaps part of that barrier she
felt come between them at all the wrong times.
When it seemed he would say no more, she came to
him and ran her fingertips gently over his flesh,
tracing the scars. "These are not from brambles.
Someone beat you."

"Yes, someone beat me," he said after an odd
pause, wondering why he couldn't keep a curb on
his tongue. He'd told Patch things he'd never even
told his best army buddies, not even when they'd sat
around saloons in Nam and gotten drunk and

maudlin, with everyone homesick and telling life stories.

"Who?" Her voice was almost inaudible.

For an instant his eyes retreated from her, his gaze turning inward....

HIS MOTHER HAD ON HER BEST DRESS, the blue one with tiny white dots. She'd been wearing her auburn hair swept atop her head like a crown, and she had refused to meet his eyes.

"Why can't I go with you, mama?"

She turned her head to look over her shoulder at the man waiting impatiently in the shiny new pickup. "You can't, that's all. I'll write to you." She touched him on his arm, then spoke to Miss Emma. "I'll send you money each week for the boy."

Miss Emma smoothed her apron over her ample stomach. "We'll be lookin' for it. Never you worry, we'll take good care of Cooper for as long as need be."

A cold fear had crept up his spine. This wasn't going to be just a weekend trip with the man like before. "When are you coming back, mama?"

"Soon's I can, Cooper, I promise."

"COOPER," PATCH SAID softly, entreatingly, and touched his arm as though he was lost. "Who beat you so?"

"Miss Emma," he said, still withdrawn into his past. "Mama left me with her when she went away. When the money stopped coming I was a burden and too small to really earn my keep."

"And when your mama came home?"

"She never did," he said in a very flat voice, remembering times when emptiness had almost overwhelmed him.

Patch heard the bitterness and knew it was etched in his soul. It was one of those little endings in life, seemingly unbearable. She was too honest to find any shallow words of comfort. "You never got over feeling abandoned by your mama, did you?"

"Look," he snapped with a trace of iron in his tone, "you asked me about the scars and I told you. There it is."

"It doesn't do any good to remember horrible things like that. It's over now."

His expression was remote, closing her out, and she knew she couldn't leave it at that. She brushed his shoulder with her fingertips, gossamer-light strokes that were a balm to his scarred flesh. Then she kissed his brow, his eyelids, his chest, until his arms came about her and they fell back on his bunk together.

In the dim light his face had a look of such intensity that it seemed to Patch everything he had left to hope or fear must be expressed there. His hands moved on her back, caressing her, his fingers cupping the sides of her breasts while his body grew hard. There was an urgency in his touch, a tension that precluded talk, even soft imprecations expressing love or desire.

Knowing he was using her flesh to blot out the pain of his past, Patch closed her eyes and gave herself up to him, her hips and thighs rising to his until they arched strongly as she joined him in the intricate ancient rhythm. His lips brushed her eyes, her cheeks, her mouth, the throbbing vein in her temple. She stroked his heaving shoulders, and his flesh piercing hers was part ecstasy, part despair. Then without warning she surrendered utterly to his spasms, and the quivering of her body drove Cooper to a swift madness, a completion. The soft guttural cry that erupted from his throat she knew she would hear forevermore in times of sadness.

Slowly, slowly their breathing quieted, yet the diminishing afterglow of sex left Patch feeling trapped somewhere between her pledge to Rosalina and reality, helpless in the presence of Cooper's splintered childhood.

She snuggled closer to him, sliding a leg over his, resting her arm across his chest so that her hand curled about the thick muscles of his far arm. He was awake, deep in thought, and she felt that instead of consoling him she had touched off his sorrow. The need to probe, to explore more fully the hurt he had suffered swept over her.

"Cooper, was there nothing you could do to stop the beatings?"

"I thought about running away." His tone was openly ironic. "I was just going on seven, so where could I have gone? How would my mother have known where to find me? I didn't know then that she wasn't coming back. When I was old enough to do a full day's work, the beatings stopped. I got cuffed now and then, but it was no worse than what my schoolmates got."

"Do you pray, Cooper?" Her voice was filled with her interest, and he felt compelled to answer against his will.

"I used to, and damned hard...."

"What was the first thing you ever prayed for, can you remember?"

He laughed, a sound devoid of humor. "Can't you guess? For my mother to come home, to come get me."

"Did you ever see her again?"

"No, never. I was in the service when she died. The Red Cross found me. The man she was living with then didn't have the money to bury her. That's all they wanted from me—money."

"Did you send it?"

"Yes."

"That's all right then." But she knew it wasn't. Her mind was caught in a tumult of ideas and sensations. She could make him happy, make him forget. She buried her face in the thick mat of golden hair on his chest. "I'm going to teach you to trap, Cooper. Teach you how to scrape fat from raw leather, how to find your way in the swamp by the sun or the stars, and I'm going to love you—"

"It won't work," he said heavily.

"It will if you want it to," she insisted fiercely. "I can't teach you to love, or to trust—that has to come from your own spirit, no? Your heart's bruised, that's all."

"I don't see it that way," he said with scorn, feeling the need to arm himself with something better than words. It was hard to change when he'd already made up his mind; hard to back away from a thing he'd resolved years ago. When Patch stiffened, he softened with a wry, mournful smile. "Be quiet, and let me make love to you."

She required a few heartbeats for herself, time to absorb, make sense of all that he had told her. "In a minute," she agreed readily, crawling over him and off the bunk to stand at the window.

The mists had risen like a gray backdrop in one overwhelming ascent, taking over the stumps of cypress, the spires of pine, the canal and its banks. Patch understood Cooper more fully now. His libido, not his heart, guided his relationships with women. The way he had been treated by his mother and Miss Emma as a child had festered like a bad sore. But sores could heal. Knowing this made her love him all the more.

The soft pounding of hooves jolted Patch from these thoughts, and across the canal a herd of small white-tailed deer broke through the dense mist, as if preparing to gallop on into the black water. But they stopped at the edge and began to drink. For a moment she wished she could join them, to eat when she was hungry, to drink when she was thirsty, to mate in season, to wander the wilderness answering only to nature. But that was fantasy. She squeezed her eyes closed tightly. Her fantasy right now was to make Cooper Vachec love her.

"You're trembling. Throw a robe or something over your shoulders so you don't get cold," he ordered, so she knew he'd been observing her. The mists parted slightly over the deer to let in light from the moon, then closed like an afterthought of God. She turned away from the scene.

"I'm just going to wash up," she said.

"Patch...."

She stopped in the middle of the room, caught in relief by moonlight that bleached the color from her flesh. With her small high breasts and the gentle rise of her ribs prominent, she appeared to Cooper to be made of the rarest porcelain. All the words he had used to describe her to himself became lost in his mind, as if the mists had intruded in his head. "I can't promise you anything. This is just something nice that happened."

There was that word again. Nice. What was between them meant everything, only Cooper would have to learn that for himself. "I know."

"Don't be long?"

"I won't."

7

"IT'S GOING TO BE A GRAND DAY!" said Patch, throwing open the door. She was wearing her old robe, her long johns underneath hugging her shapely calves. "It's going to be a saffron sun, a good-luck omen. The air is just right for setting traps."

Cooper felt the first draft of icy air and burrowed deeper under the counterpane, though he kept an attentive eye on Patch. There was a little catch in her voice, a new softness in her dark flashing eyes, an exhilaration of spirit due to more than awakened desire or satisfied senses. "You've been looking forward to today, haven't you?" he said.

She smiled at him, then turned away and gazed out over the swamp, almost as if she was seeking the answer to give him. Her eyes alighted on scrub oak, towering pines and willow brush, with cypress etched in skeletal outlines above the black flowing water. She was reminded of the deer she'd seen. "I have been waiting, and wanting it to come. It's like when you know you're going to get a present—you even know what it is—and still the anticipation of it fills you with excitement. I feel something bubbly inside that won't be pushed down."

"Could be gas."

Patch laughed. "Being a man, you would say that." The bayou caught the reflection of the rising sun, lifting riotously in the east. She sighed happily. "I don't understand how anyone who's lived here would ever go away."

"I have an itchy foot," Cooper said. "No one place is home to me."

Patch took his words to heart, but the little pang they caused didn't make her fret. She moved from the doorway where the frostiness of the air had touched her glowing skin. "If you want to see a real trapper at work you better crawl out of that bed. Breakfast in ten minutes."

"THERE!" She pointed to a scrubby willow, stripped of leaves by the wind. "Ease up to that stump."

Following her hand signals, Cooper guided the putt-putt until, nimble-footed even with clumsy rubber boots, Patch leaped over a jumble of traps in the prow to the soggy bank. She stood for a minute, studying muskrat mounds on the quarter acre of bog. "It'll carry ten traps easily."

Cooper knew the drill now. Count out the traps from the bottom of the putt-putt, the same number of cane poles to mark the trap sites from the pirogue that was hauled behind on a dragline. Then follow precisely in Patch's footsteps or find himself up to his thighs in mud.

"Nutria make their home in abandoned muskrat mounds, but they spend most of their time in the water, so we'll stake traps on canal banks. For that we don't have to get out of the boat," Patch said when the last muskrat trap had been set.

She watched for nutria sign, pointing out to Cooper the bent swamp grass and travel-worn mud slicks. In each site she set a trap and drove a pole deep into the mud, and they moved quickly on to the next.

At one point she touched him on the shoulder. "You wanted to know what a nutria looks like. There's one now." A rodent, ugly as sin, was poised for escape, standing up on its hindquarters. It had orange buckteeth, webbed feet on short legs, a scaly tail and thick brown fur. "A twelve-pounder," Patch said. The animal caught their scent and dived into the shallow canal.

"They can swim?"

"Like fish, and stay under water as long as an otter. The State brought them up from South America to eat the water hyacinths choking the bayous, but they prefer swamp grass. And they breed... well, like rats."

"Rat fur? You make money on rat fur?"

"Nutria pelts," she corrected. "Used in Europe for utility furs to line jackets, boots, that sort of thing."

"How much do you get per pelt?" He cursed his interest but listened attentively.

"Depends on the market. There've been years when we got as high as twelve dollars for prime, and others when we were happy to see fifty cents. If we get four dollars a pelt this season...." Her voice trailed off with unguarded hope.

"Chancy business, then, isn't it?"

"No more than any other, prob'ly. A pair of trappers willing to work can pull thirty thousand dollars in a season—cash. Which reminds me. Turn into that deep creek. I want to check the hoop net."

"Thirty thousand dollars in three or four months?" Cooper muttered incredulously. "I have to work all year to make that."

She dropped him a glance. "You have to look at things straight. There're expenses to be paid out of that—food, fuel, lease, licenses, boat upkeep, equipment. It eats up capital.... There's catfish, too. They earn about the same, and no fishing on Sunday, either." She sighed wistfully. "Then there's shrimping late spring and early fall, but we lost our shrimp boat when papa drowned. I'm wise about money because papa taught me, and some say I learned more than he had to teach. I'm very practical, I know how to parcel it out, and if it wasn't for Rosalina's medical expenses, I'd have replaced the shrimp boat by now."

For a moment Cooper's attractive face looked worn down, eroded. He said abruptly, "You're hanging out bait for me, aren't you? Trying to appeal to my greed. I wouldn't take a crying dime from a woman."

"*Grand-mère* says greed is universal, so I don't see how you or anyone can avoid it." Her eyes shone. "Though I wouldn't want a partner unless he wanted me first, money second, and he'd darn sure have to earn his share. He *would* earn his share. And I don't suppose that means any man I'd take up with would have to pocket his pride. Besides, all the money I earn right now is for Rosalina, so I guess a man would just have to want me for myself." She shoved the last cane pole into the mud, set the trap and sat down on the prow thwart. "That's the last one. Let's head back to camp."

Patch could not have imagined a more helpful partner than Cooper. No matter that he was unskilled and that she had to keep an eye on him for safety's sake. He had melded smoothly into the routine of working the traps, walking the bog and handling the putt-putt, no mean feat with the pirogue trailing behind, trying to get itself snagged on every submerged stump. He was uncomplaining about the weather, too. You could tell so much about a man watching how he handled himself in the swamp. If he was rash, or careless, or a laggard—there it all lay before you, revealed in a day or less, as surely as if you had reached in and pulled it out of his soul for all to see.

For his part, Cooper admired Patch's skill and knowledge, and thought, even bundled up against the cold, she was lithe and vivacious in a quaint country way. He had caught the excitement that possessed her all day, and it had felt good to be working with his hands. Gazing at Patch, half-obsessed, he saw her all at once sprawled on his bunk, naked, her hair in wild disarray, her tiny pink nipples standing erect from their darker areoles. He could, if he closed his eyes, feel her swaying toward him in the moonlight, entranced and suppliant.

"I don't know what you're thinking on," Patch said quickly. "But if you don't veer off left we're going to be spending all night digging ourselves out of a mud flat."

Cooper opened his eyes, jerked on the throttle wire, and the boat passed the hazard—by inches. "Sorry," he muttered sheepishly.

"It's okay. Were you thinking about me?" She started rewinding her muffler about her neck, as he had turned the boat into the sharp, cold wind.

"Why would I do that?" he answered, neither denying nor admitting it.

"Because we haven't had a chance to make love all day, and I thought what with you having the kind of appetite for sex you do, that—" Her hands flew to her mouth. "I didn't mean anything nasty by that, Cooper, so don't go looking at me like you're a storm fixing to swoop down the chimney. Don't say I'm not a nice girl, either. I'm French, and the French are romantic."

He gave a disparaging shake of his head while the warm and vital presence of Patch before him mingled with the lingering vision in his mind. "I've been blind, but now I see," he said dryly.

Patch brightened. She heard no sting in his words. "*Bien.* That sounds like a hymn *grand-mère* hums sometimes."

"Count it as a prayer."

She leaned forward, her dark eyes wide and pure. "An asking prayer or a thanking one?"

He laughed. "You're incorrigible. Now turn around on that thwart and guide me into that next mud trough you call a canal. I can't see where to turn because of the rushes hanging over now that the tide's running."

The happy warmth Patch felt as she did his bidding went bone deep, and not a little of it settled in her thighs with ebullient anticipation.

That same night, after their supper of fried catfish found trapped in the hoop net, crisp potatoes, hush puppies and sliced tomatoes with mayonnaise, Patch propped her elbow on the scarred table and sank a moment into reflection.

It had been a year and a day ago that Rosalina had been scalded. She couldn't help thinking that if she'd hired a partner instead of allowing her sister to help, there wouldn't be the sense of a family divided that sometimes plagued her. Not that she was about to cry over spilled milk. And mama couldn't help the way she was, having had to worry about Rosalina before she'd even come out of mourning for papa. But if the accident hadn't happened, Patch herself wouldn't have her promise to Rosalina to contend with.... She didn't think she would have married Arlis. By and by she would have caught on to his lazy ways. Still, she had a qualm that she *might* have been married before she had met Cooper.

The scratch of a match on pumice brought her back to the present. Cooper was looking at her through spiraling cigarette smoke. "You were off somewhere," he said.

"Just thinking," she answered rather wistfully. "There's still some daylight left. I think I'll work on the putt-putt's motor. It had a clink in it today I hadn't noticed before, and the last thing I need is for that motor to go out on me when I got a load of carcasses to drag up.''

"You got a hammer and nails handy? I could attach that skinning table to the shed wall better. It shook a bit when we got out the rope to pull the pirogue. I used to do carpentry work on the farm. I've forgotten a good share of it, but I think I could remember enough to fix the latch on the shed door, too, so you don't have to prop it closed with a board.''

"Arlis promised he'd get around to fixing that for me.''

"Well, Arlis isn't here, is he?''

"No, and I can't say I'm disappointed,'' she answered with feeling.

"Don't go getting any ideas about my helping you,'' Cooper cautioned. "I just need to work off that supper, and I can't go for a walk without finding myself up to my neck in mud.''

"I've done all the thinking I've a mind to do today,'' she said majestically, and went to find the hammer. He'd be mighty surprised, she thought with a secret little smile, if she reached inside her shirt and handed him the one that was pounding on her heart.

"ARE YOU HAPPY, COOPER?''

"What kind of a question is that?'' he answered warily.

"One I wish you'd answer. Are you happy being here with me?'' They had worked around the camp until full dark, then had come inside, washing up the dishes while fresh coffee dripped.

"I don't want that kind pressure, Patch. Stop it.''

"You talk as if you've always been grown up, never about your youth. Were you a naughty little boy?''

"You know I didn't have much of a youth."

"Before your mother left, I mean. You had good times with her, no?"

"I was seven when my mother went away, and I was born in the root cellar during a tornado that killed my dad and older brother. I don't remember much in between, except that we were cramped in winter and moved pallets out-of-doors in spring and summer." He spoke harshly, as though discovering something distasteful on his tongue and wishing to spit it out.

"You say 'mother' like you would a bad word. You remember good things before you were seven, but you just don't want to admit it. You've never forgiven her for going off, leaving you, and not coming back to get you. Remembering only the bad gives you license to hate. That's what you've survived on prob'ly—hate."

His hand shot out, grasping hers, squeezing until she winced. "You've gone too far this time with your prying. What and how I survived is not any of your business, and quit trying to make it so. I'm happy! Does that suit you?"

"You're hurting me, and you sound about as happy as a pen full of sows watching a boar get butchered."

He loosened his grip, but didn't release her hand. "Stop trying to mold me into something I'm not."

"You said you wanted to help; I let you. You wanted to make love to me, and I let you do that, too. Whatever you're made up of is so stiff I couldn't bend or mold it with a brazier and a hammer."

"That's not what I meant and you know it." She had such a woebegone look on her face that he lifted her hand to his lips and kissed each finger. "I didn't mean to hurt you."

Consoled, Patch became conscious of a rousing in her blood. "You're too melancholy, Cooper."

Shrugging, he let go of her hand, lit a cigarette and pulled the smoke deep into his lungs.

"We're all that way when we find something we want and can't keep." He couldn't blame her for the old raw wounds connected to his childhood, and he chastized himself for behaving like an ass. Without conscious thought he knew he was as much afraid of being loved as he was of loving. Yet he was succumbing to a madness that kept him savoring rare feelings and dangerous sensations; if he let himself go he would be taking an emotional long shot. Yet the thought of a future time when he couldn't have Patch stirred the heat in his groin. "Is that coffee ready yet?"

"It's ready, and I'll pour it. But you just want to change the subject."

After she passed him the can of Pet milk and the sugar, she leaned on the sink, looking out. Low ground mist glistened in the starlight, and the black sky and white mist seemed united in luminosity. Usually such a sight would have uplifted Patch, but Cooper and his stubborn ways obsessed her now.

The light over the table flickered and dimmed.

Patch blinked, her lashes lying on her cheek like tiny dark crescents. "Generator's running out of fuel. I guess I forgot to fill it." She reached for her jacket.

"Don't worry with it now," he called, his voice unbearably soft.

"But I can hear the generator choking...." Huge and liquid, her eyes suddenly filled with clarity and her throat tightened.

The bulb flickered once more and died. In the dark their bodies were shadows of substance; only the glow of Cooper's cigarette was clearly visible. His voice dropped to the edge of sound. "I want you so badly right now, I can taste it."

Patch waited in interminable time, then leaned slowly toward him, toward the glowing end of the cigarette. "I want you, too," she breathed in in a whisper. "I ought not to, but...."

He moved from the table, began taking off his clothes. Patch did the same, and then his hands were circling her impossibly small waist as though to make certain she was mortal flesh.

"Shouldn't we bathe first?" she managed. The inch of space between them closed. His knees touched hers, his arms enveloped her, pulling her close so that there was no doubt of his arousal, and then the tips of her breasts met the silken hair on his chest and Patch nearly swooned.

"Later," he said. Bathing was the furthest thing from his mind. With a trembling finger he traced the curve of her spine. "Lovely back... lovely... everything...." He trailed kisses on her temple where a tiny vein pulsated, nibbled her earlobe, pressed his lips into the sweet-scented hollows of her throat until Patch moaned with erotic delight.

"We're going to stand here in the middle of the room all night prob'ly?" she whispered in a low passionate voice.

"No...we're not," Cooper replied, and Patch's attention was diverted by his fingertips making feather-light forays on the sides of her breasts and over the soft slight roundness of her belly as he sought the source of her ecstasy.

"My legs are getting rubbery," she moaned, and her stance broke just a little. He picked her up and carried her to his bed, and there were no more words between them for a long, long while as they joined in a world where no words were necessary.

COOPER STROKED Patch's soft inner thigh. "Are you asleep?"

"No, *m'sieu*."

He smiled into silky fragrant curls at the insouciance in her voice. "Do you believe in sorcery?"

Patch crossed herself quickly. *"Aliéné!"* she cried, calling him a lunatic. "I only believe in God, His son, His mother and all the saints—and sometimes, Monsignor Burns."

He laughed. "And do you pray to all of them?"

To Father Burns I only talk. I pray to all the others, but of course, one must be careful how one addresses God."

"Because I ended up on your doorstep instead of someone else?" He wasn't accepting, just teasing.

"A tiny oversight for which I've forgiven Him. You're wonderful and strong like Cajun men, only better." Her fingers moved in lazy circles over his chest and stomach and felt the muscles grow taut. She loved having this power over Cooper's body. It was awesome in its way, and the awe drove her to say the words. She couldn't swallow them back because the rush of emotion following them tightened her vocal cords, leaving her tongue to clatter on its own. "I love you, Cooper. I love you more than anyone I've ever known."

His heart skipped a beat, then raced wildly. He didn't believe it for a minute but found himself hoping. Hope—that amorphous thing on which he'd wasted most of his life. For a moment he lay motionless, as if all his strength was spent, and he didn't know how to gather his forces together again. Wishing for things had never done him one particle of good. If he'd learned a single thing in his thirty-three years, it was that.

Patch sensed him pulling slightly away from her, and her limbs trembled as his silence went on and on. "Did you hear what I said?" she echoed hoarsely, staring at him, watching feverishly for a hint of how he was feeling.

Starlight streamed in the window over his bunk, and he could see how tightly the skin was drawn across her cheekbones. "I heard."

"Aren't you going to say it back to me?"

"No."

A low moan of despair escaped her lips, and a savage anger borne of hurt shot through her. Curling her small hands into fists, she pounded his chest. "Oh, I take it back! I take everything back! I take back my body! My dream. I ask God to erase my prayer!"

It took Cooper several stunned seconds to fend off her fists, which were doing no damage. A great surge of emotion, the most overwhelming sensation he had ever experienced in his life, began to grow in him. It made the skin on the back of his neck prickle, made blood pulse hotly through his veins, made his tongue so thick he could barely shape words. He caught her in his arms and crushed her close so that she had no room to maneuver and lay shuddering in his arms.

"Don't take it back," he heard himself say above the roaring in his ears. "Don't take it back—"

"I do take it back." Patch felt the tremor that went through him, knowing that he was suffering something her befuddled mind could not name. He was touching her, caressing her feverishly, building between them a mounting passion that demanded surfeit. It was a dangerous dark passion on the edge of a chasm, and she felt herself falling as his lips begged succor from hers. The rising between his thighs was an engorged being, thrusting into her, impaling her, possessing her, as though every inch of her flesh were being dissolved into his and she could never retrieve that which she had given to him.

Just when she thought she could bear no more, a

rapture such as she'd never experienced took hold, scoring every nerve with an exquisite agony, suspending her by a gossamer thread above an earth gone wild with carnal joy. Then the thread stretched with her weight, down...down...until she drifted into an engulfing darkness.

When she wakened it was to find Cooper bending over her with a wet cloth, bathing her face by the glow of a kerosene lantern kept for emergencies. The wick had not been trimmed and the flame was uneven, skittering inside its chimney so that tongues of light seemed to dance across the ceiling. He had on an old brown terry robe and a pair of slippers she had not seen before—another of the treasures he kept pulling from his bottomless duffel.

"If I've hurt you, I couldn't live with myself," he told her, his voice unsteady, when he saw her eyes were open. That look she had seen on his face earlier seemed locked in place. A boundary had been crossed into a new land, one in which she didn't know the terrain.

She felt immeasurably weak. "I'm not hurt. I think I fainted, but I've never fainted before in my life, so I couldn't say for sure."

He dropped the washcloth into the dishpan, then helped her into clean long johns. Patch felt suddenly awkward and off balance, the dizzy feeling coming stronger as he gathered her in his arms and carried her to her own bunk.

Confusion welled up inside her. "You don't want me in your bed?"

"I want it too much, too hard...too savagely. What happened...it was like a dam bursting inside of me," and she knew it was true, because there was still a hunger concealed in his eyes. He was going to examine it, analyze it, pick it apart until reason reasserted itself.

She touched his hand, tracing its shape. "This has moved on parts of me that no other man has ever touched or seen. That has to count for something."

"It does. I'm not trying to make light of what we've done or how much it meant to me." There was a kind of thin panic in his voice. Patch grappled with it and finally placed it. She'd heard that tone only once before—when papa had been bitten by a water snake. It had taken him death-defying seconds to find the snake in the scrub and discover it wasn't poisonous. Still he had been feverish, his eyes burning until they had taken on a flat look, like Cooper's now.

She felt her mouth going dry. "Will you be leaving, then?" She didn't mean right that minute, only that when he did go, it would be forever.

A muscle leaped as he held his jaw rigid. "I don't know." He pulled the quilts up to her chin. "Sleep now."

"Sleep? A person can't sleep with her whole life falling down around her ears."

Cooper looked infinitely pained. "I've never met anyone whose world had more solid foundations even though it's built on mud and water."

"You think that counts now?"

"Yes, and you do, too."

He moved away to gather up the dishpan and put it with a clatter on the old wooden sink. Then he brought the kerosene lantern to the table, where he sat down to brood over a glass of whiskey.

Patch paid scant attention to the ceiling, but after a while her eyes shifted, taking in the room, as if observing it for the very first time. There were the deer antlers marching unevenly across the wooden walls, holding her robe, extra long johns, slickers so supple and worn that gray rubber showed through; her guns, the .22 and .410, standing in the corner with the broom that fitted her sweeping stroke just right; the old sofa, its cover once red and scratchy, but because of use now smooth to touch. Lastly there was the old windup clock on the stove that was keeping time so sharply, yet year in and year out it kept no time at all from the end of one trapping season until the beginning of the next, being left to tick away into oblivion when she closed up camp. She loved the old shack too much to be troubled by its flaws and didn't take them into account.

Her eyes alighted on Cooper, sitting at the table where she and papa had so often played cards or dominos on rain-chased days. A lump formed in her throat, but she held her gaze steady, aware peripherally of the uneven lamp flame, its pungent odor and the fragrance of the apples in the bowl mingling with the leftover smell of fried fish. The camp wasn't much, but it was part of her life, and it belonged wholly to her. And there she had allowed Cooper to come into it and make her feel all raggedy inside. Why, it should be Cooper in bed sulking, not her!

A hot wave of resentment swept over her for the impertinence this represented on the part of an outsider. She threw back the quilts in a purposeful way, put on her robe and crossed the room with the kind of grace that comes with a natural stride and the light-footedness of a skilled hunter.

She felt Cooper's eyes boring into her and glanced covertly at him, seeing something akin to appeal in his troubled eyes. He looked so self-controlled and so lost that she felt a pang of sympathy and almost turned back to her bunk. But she had something she had to say to him.

She heated coffee, standing with her back to him until she had filled her cup, then turned to face him. He lifted his head, looking at her, a haunted look.

"I love you, Cooper. It's really no business of

yours that I do or don't. A person doesn't have to
have permission to love. What you seem to want is a
woman who's ashamed to come right out and say
yes out loud. If I told you no, I didn't like making
love, or if I pretended I didn't, I'd be obliged to keep
saying it, prob'ly."

She filled her lungs. "You're all mixed up about
what a nice girl is. I say my prayers, do my work and
take care of my family. I don't know if that makes
me nice, but it doesn't make me bad. I know I don't
feel like what we've been doing is a sin, and I
wouldn't tell it in confession come Easter.

"You've got something driving you because you
feel forsaken by your mother. You think she was bad
because she went off with a man. But you don't
think it's bad for a man to go off with a woman. I
don't want to call you names, but you're selfish, and
maybe two-faced." The realization crossed her mind
that she would only lose in the end if she sought to
force the issue further now. Her rounded little chin
tilted forward, expressing a pride that was an es-
sence of her being. "I love you. I like making love
with you, but I won't come begging just to make you
feel good. That's all I got to say."

Her nerves seemed to absorb every tiny sound—
the rush of wind around the eaves, the faraway hoot
of an owl. She imagined that she could even hear the
soft susurrus of the mists as they glided over the surface of the bayou. She put her cup down on the sink.
"Well, maybe I got one more thing to say," she added gravely. "I can't love me for you. It takes up all
the space in my heart just to love you, and there's
barely room left for *maman*, *grand-mère* and Rosalina. If papa was alive... well, that doesn't matter. If
he was, we wouldn't have had all those opportuni-
ties for pettin' parties. You ought to know, in case
that's what's keeping you here, that there won't be

any more. Even if there'd be time, I won't do it with you again. It wouldn't seem right now, with me declaring and you not."

Cooper waited until she was tucked into her bed before he spoke. He didn't say anything earth shattering. He couldn't. His emotions were bridled, bound tightly with invisible steel and buried in his gut. "That was quite a speech."

"It came on me that I had to say it." She closed her eyes and brushed her curls back with both hands. Her body felt sore from their lovemaking, but she kept it to herself. "I'm going to sleep now. Sunup'll be here before you know it."

No matter how sharply he reviewed it, Cooper couldn't find much wrong with what Patch had said. She knew what she wanted and wasn't afraid to go after it. He knew what he wanted, too, or didn't want—he didn't want it to end. But a lifetime of protecting himself from hurt couldn't be swept away overnight. Patch was a trapper all right. He was squirming.

8

"HOW COME YOU'RE LAYING ABED so late in the morning? You sick?"

Sleepily Patch cracked open an eyelid, looking at Arlis Lafargue through slitted lashes as he bent over her bunk. The edge of her sleep-drugged mind recognized the sound of rain lashing the camp's tin roof. She groaned at such bad luck on the first day of harvesting and wanted nothing more than to roll over and return to her dreams, as dissatisfying as they had been. "I'm not sick," she said thickly, though as she stretched she ached from head to toe. "What are you doing here, Arlis?"

Before he had a chance to answer, Cooper burst through the back door, shedding rain from a slicker and carrying a bucket of bayou water. He stopped dead, coldly taking in the tableau of Arlis leaning over Patch. His face was gaunt from lack of sleep, his disposition as worn as his face looked. "Didn't hear your boat over the storm, Lafargue. Why don't you stand outside until Patch makes herself decent for company?"

Arlis pivoted. "Aw, it's wet out yonder. Besides Patch and I, we're old—"

"Please." The single word was unmistakably a command. Arlis hesitated. Cooper shrugged out of the rain gear and hung it on the antler by the back door where it sent rivulets of water cascading over the faded green linoleum. He sauntered toward Patch, gathering up her pants and shirt as he went

and tossing them across her bunk, then stood with
his hands on his hips and a slight smile of owner-
ship on his face until Arlis, grumbling beneath his
breath, went out into the rain.

Patch threw off the bedclothes and pulled on her
pants. Piqued, though she would have done the
same, she said, "You didn't have any right to do
that."

"You have rights, I have rights," Cooper noted,
bringing to surface all that had gone between them
the previous night.

She looked at him, a silky gleam in her eye. "This
is my camp. I'll decide who stays in and who goes
out, and you can't go acting like you have say so
over me. You don't."

"I know the look in a man's eye when he wants a
woman," Cooper replied icily. "Lafargue has that
look. He was going to say you two are old friends.
He meant more than friends, didn't he?"

"No more so than you and your landlady. Your
past is all bunched up inside you, prob'ly mine is,
too, in some ways," she added to be fair. "You don't
like prying, I don't like prying."

"That tells me more than you think."

"Maybe it tells you I'm a nice girl," she said, ignoring his thunderous look. Buttoning her shirt,
tucking it in, rolling up the sleeves, slipping her feet
into moccasins took only a moment. Her eyebrows
rose in a delicate curve, giving her face an innocent
open expression, one far more trenchant than sarcasm. She folded her arms across her breasts like the
sculpted effigy on a tomb and asked sweetly, "Decent enough for you now?"

"Yes." He glared at her, strode to the door and,
yanking it open, called a dripping Arlis inside.

While Cooper moved around her pouring coffee,
Patch washed her face, brushed her teeth and hair,

groping for an understanding of Cooper's mood. Stiff-necked jealousy of Arlis, she decided. Yet, unbidden, he put coffee in front of their guest. Courtesy won out; she liked that about a man.

"How's Una making out?" she asked as she picked up her own coffee and blew on it.

"She'd be fine if she had some sugar," Arlis answered. "We run out."

Patch frowned with a touch of indignation, though she bit it back. She made a resolution to match Cooper's courtesy, which she noted did not extend to joining them at the table. Remote, bullish, he was drinking his coffee standing up, watching her and Arlis. An undercurrent began to build between the two men, of tension and of something more.... Trouble was hounding her enough without jealousy fueling the situation. Besides, she didn't care about Arlis and Una anymore. "I've a two-pound bag to spare," she said, and when neither man spoke, improvised a neutral topic. "Hate this wet coming up right at the front of the season, but the rain barrel was low so it evens out prob'ly."

Cooper's dark lofty expression didn't change. Patch sighed inwardly, and got up to get the sugar. "I have shed work to do until the rain stops," she announced, hoping Arlis would take the hint and go.

"Speaking of shed work," he began, not budging, "high tide came up and floated away my cane poles. You got any to spare?"

Her resolution broke around the edges. "First ice, now sugar and site poles... why didn't you see to all that before you went to camp?"

"I thought you and me would be trapping partners. You never out and out said we wouldn't."

"I haven't said ten words to you in months, Arlis Lafargue, until you sashayed up to my wharf last week!"

Shooting a glance at Cooper, Arlis's lips curved slyly. "Didn't expect you'd be holding Una against me after all this time, no?"

Patch clenched her hands about her cup until they were almost bloodless. "I don't hold Una against anything. Most prob'ly she's better than you deserve. Take the sugar and what poles you need from under the camp. If you need anything else, make a trip into Catahoula."

"You used to be a lot more friendly," Arlis complained, aiming a sour look at Cooper as though this turn of events were all his fault.

"I used to be a lot of things I'm not anymore. Stupid is one of them. Now get out of here, and next time, you knock before you come barging into my camp."

Arlis tucked the sugar under his coat and rose to leave. His eyes tracked Cooper. "Heard tell you hired Patch as a guide. If she don't work out, you can send word to me. I can guide you as well or better."

"I'm pleased with Patch. But I'll keep you in mind. Are you as organized about guide work as you are about trapping?"

"Are you making a slur on me, *m'sieu*?" Arlis asked, fingering the knife at his belt.

"Just asking," Cooper replied blandly, but Patch saw his muscles bunch as if he was ready to spring, and noted the tight line of his lips. She grabbed the Cajun by his shirt sleeve, half dragging, half pushing him toward the door.

"You've overstayed your welcome, Arlis. If you're in a mood to fight, look up one of your lazy brothers. They'll oblige you, no doubt."

Long minutes later, hunched beneath a tarpaulin, Arlis moved off down the bayou in his boat, while the rain slammed across the swamp in pitiless intensity, obscuring stumps and trees alike.

Patch stood just inside the threshold, the rain spattering her lightly, watching Arlis until he disappeared from sight. She discovered Cooper standing diffidently behind her, staring at her in a strange way, and she had the feeling he was appraising her, as if what he wanted from her might be both too much and not enough. "It had to warm up to rain," she said inanely, shifting her weight. "I guess it'll really turn cold when it stops."

"I could have handled Lafargue—you didn't have to interfere. I don't hide behind a woman's skirt."

"If you're spoiling for a fight, Cooper Vachec, I'll fight you!"

He retreated hastily, aware that he was treading on somewhat delicate ground. Patch seemed overnight to have acquired a strange new stateliness that made her less approachable than before. He had created an estrangement between them by not mouthing the words she wanted to hear. Perhaps she'd said all on that score that she meant to, but he knew the memory of it was still in her mind. Damn his pride! But he couldn't just shrug it off like an old sweater; he'd lived with it, depended upon it too long. He felt as if a heavy weight had settled on his shoulders, bending them to the breaking point. He glanced over at Patch and caught her watchful gaze—measuring his misery, he thought resentfully, and his pride constricted him like a steel vise. It took him a moment to find the question he'd meant to ask when she had awakened. "How do you feel this morning?" There was concern in his voice, and strain.

"I'm fine, stronger than I look," she said with a delicate archness. She would have to be, because she didn't think her sexuality, now that it had been aroused so riotously, could lie fallow and dormant for very long. Even the elements were against her, with the rain enclosing the camp like a seductive velvet curtain.

Cooper touched her arm. She jerked away as though burned. He looked shocked, his eyes reflecting volatile thoughts, his features doubt. "I did hurt you last night. I was so out of control...."

"In some ways, yes."

"Let's have coffee and talk for a few minutes."

"You have something you wish to say to me?"

He sighed heavily. "No, not anything particular. I just don't...can't bear the way you're acting. I feel like you're eluding me, which is a funny thing to say because you can't, you know, not in this room."

"No, not in this room. But in my heart—"

"You're beginning to sound as formal as Natalie."

"Well, *maman* does have a charm and dignity that you can't quarrel with, no?" She stepped back and closed the door on the rain. "I think I will have that coffee, and breakfast, too, while we're at it. The wind's shifting, coming out of the north and pushing the rain to the Gulf, so I'll be running my traps later today after all."

"I'll go with you."

"Running traps isn't for the squeamish or the fainthearted."

"I'll pull my weight. You just tell me what to do."

Eventually she agreed to let him go with her. At day's end he would be worn out and so would she. Her heart suddenly contracted torturously as she thought about love and loving, the wondrous glory in it and the awful anxiety. Today there would be no waiting with impatience for night to come, no reunion spontaneously sought and voluptuously prolonged. It didn't feel so good, this standing on the majesty of principle, thought Patch.

THE BOGS WERE ENVELOPED in ragged drifts of undulating mists, and though the rain had stopped, gray clouds lay low over the wild and lonely swamp so that Patch could not tell where in the distance the mists left off and the sky began.

Cooper turned from the prow thwart to say through stiffened lips, "It's colder than charity out here!"

"I warned you to wear two pairs of underwear. We can't turn back now. It always turns off cold after a rain, especially in winter."

"I didn't ask you to turn back."

No, you didn't, she thought, *so you'll suffer the cold.* She hated it that he would have to, but harvesting the traps was her uppermost priority now, each pelt counting in the tally, adding up to dollars needed desperately. "If you'll come back here and work the rudder wire, I'll take the prow. It'll be easier for me to get to the traps from there."

They exchanged places, and despite the despair Patch felt over Cooper, a jubilant sense of well-being welled up in her as they approached the first trap. She dispatched the nutria with her stun stick, released it from the trap, tossed it into the bottom of the boat, reset the trap and with a grin said, "Go on to the next."

There were no nutria in the next trap or the next, nor any muskrat at all in the half a hundred traps she had placed atop the marsh ground. The hundred fifty nutria traps yielded only nineteen carcasses. Her face was sharp with cold when she stepped into the boat for the last time, empty-handed. It was a horrible moment, and she had to swallow back the tears. "Let's go back to camp. Something's wrong."

She said it not with the lilting tone Cooper was so used to, but like a weary old woman would. "Maybe you should have used some bait," he suggested, torn because she was so obviously dejected.

If she could have, Patch would have smiled. "The animals aren't wary yet like they sometimes get toward the end of the season," she declared angrily. "Three-quarters of my traps should have been full."

They were eating a supper she had prepared, and Cooper was stirring his round on his plate, looking for a potato that wasn't hard in the middle and pulling apart chicken legs to find them half-raw. Patch's mind had not been on food, wasn't on food now, and Cooper didn't think it would be for a good long while. "I'm not in the mood for chicken," he advanced cautiously. "Mind if I make a ham sandwich?"

"I've been taken by a poacher. Brave little bugger," she said contemptuously. "He thought I wouldn't work my traps because of the rain, so he ran them for me. If I don't stop him, he'll keep right on, prob'ly."

"What'll you do?"

"Catch him at it, that's what," she replied softly. "He'll run my traps tonight, too, soon as it's dark, but he'll be selective, keeping to traps set along the deeper canals on the outer edge of my lease. He'll be working in a boat with a heavy motor that's got some speed, just in case, to make a fast getaway. He won't be using lights, but I'll be able to hear that motor." She got up and looked out the door. "No moon tonight. Good for him and good for me."

"You can't be serious about going back out there in the dark, not to mention that it's colder than blazes. Do you want a sandwich?"

"I'm not afraid of the dark. I know every inch of this bayou, and I can dress against the cold." Her eyes grew hard. "I hate a thief about as much as I do a government man. How would you like it if you went to your mailbox to pick up your paycheck and found someone had taken it? Rosalina needs fur money for her operation. That poacher as good as lifted my paycheck!"

"There are agencies to help with Rosalina's care—"

"Charity!" she blazed, nearly choking on the word. "I know a family that took it once, and after a while they couldn't hold their heads up. They weren't ashamed of being poor, it was just the welfare worker, dressed all neat and tidy, kept looking on them with suspicion, demeaning them. They kept toadying to her and strangling on it. That's what defeated them." She shook her head of dark curls disgustedly, and the memory brought on another. "One winter trapping was off, and poachers were coming at us from every side. *Maman* needed new shoes and a leg brace that year, and papa was in a mood—death-scared, because he'd been bitten by a snake the summer before and the worry of it lingered. He made me promise on my honor that if anything ever happened to him, I'd never take charity and I wouldn't let *maman* take it, either, because sometimes she can't smell the difference in money." She looked at Cooper suddenly, sharply. "Don't you ever mention those agencies to *maman*."

"I didn't understand a word you said. You know I don't understand French."

"Oh." She had to say it all over in English.

"Surely Natalie's pride is as great as yours," Cooper offered soothingly after Patch had translated.

"She took your money, didn't she? Government money?"

"It's not tainted, you know." His voice was soft but reproachful.

"Most prob'ly is," she returned glumly, and moved away from the table to the guns that stood in the corner by the broom.

Cooper stopped building his ham sandwich and looked at her grimly. "What's on your mind with those guns?"

"Shooting a poacher."

"Oh, good crying damn!" he uttered quietly. "You can't just go out and kill somebody. You can't take the law into your own hands! So somebody tripped a few of your traps. There's always tomorrow."

She turned her eyes on him, and they were glowing coals of ebony. "Robbing two hundred traps is more than a few, but I'll wait for the sheriff. You go call him up. How long do you reckon it'll take for him to get here?"

He emitted a low groan. "Patch, I can't let you do this."

She broke open the shotgun and inserted two shells, closing the gun with a harsh snap. It looked like a cannon in her tiny slim hands. "I don't see how you can stop me, *m'sieu.*"

His eyes turned cold, but not from fear, nor did he look away, but gave a small nod. Her breathing was silent, her cheekbones prominent under taut, wind-reddened skin, and there was a slight frown on her brow. She looked so frail, his heart twisted. "I'll say one thing for you, you're a mighty determined woman."

What Cooper couldn't see was her dry throat and her body aching for him. Oh, there were times, Patch thought, when pride was only compensation for defeat.

"Is that better than being nice, Cooper?"

"YOU DON'T HAVE TO GO with me. I may be all night, till dawn anyway, and like you said, it's cold."

"I doubled up on my long johns. Besides, somebody has to protect you."

"You? From the swamp? From a poacher who

doesn't expect me?'' Her voice was laced with incredulity.

"From yourself.'' He could almost bring himself to believe that he could protect her from any danger, any hurt, but he knew she wouldn't allow it. He longed to touch her, to hold her—to feel her warmth. To be warm! Which was no small thing, he was coming to learn. He handed her the thermos of hot coffee and stepped carefully into the pirogue. "I can help you pole.''

"Did you fill up the generator like I asked? I want those lights burning bright in case he's checking.''

"To the brim.''

"Push off then.''

The wind clamped its icy jaws around them and sucked them into its frigid gut. The moon stayed hidden behind dark clouds, and bits and pieces of marsh and bog blended together with the darker water of the canals they traveled. The only sound was the soft suck and splash of the push poles as first Cooper, then Patch drove them through the water and into the mud to propel the pirogue. Startled from its sleep beneath a willow as the sturdy craft brushed past, a gull flew alongside, its hoarse squawk eerie and hollow in the dark. "Get out of here!'' Patch whispered, and it flew off.

Cold minutes turned into frozen hours as they patrolled the outer edges of the lease. Cooper craved a smoke, but Patch talked him out of it. "A coffee break instead?'' he called very softly, careful not to lift his voice above the wind.

Patch laid her pole across the prow. "Yes. I can't hear anything over your chattering teeth anyway.''

She sat still, listening. "Wait!'' she whispered. She had heard a sound, the snap of a trap as it closed, perhaps a carcass hitting the bottom of a boat with a thud. Then she discerned the tiny pinprick of light as it flared red and faded seventy yards distant. She lifted the shotgun to her shoulder, lean muscles tensing for action, no breath in a pounding chest, and waited until the poacher took another drag on his cigarette. She sited on the glow as he lowered it in an arc and squeezed very gently, very determinedly, both triggers.

"Good crying damn!" shouted Cooper as the swamp exploded in gunfire, and the thermos leaped from his hands. He dived for Patch, the blast ringing in his ears. The slender pirogue rocked dangerously. "I didn't believe you'd really do it!"

Across the black water came the sound of a grunt, a motor being started, missing, catching and the roar as it churned away into the distance.

Patch went rigid at Cooper's touch. "I didn't do it good enough," she said dejectedly. "He got away."

Cooper didn't know whether to laugh or cry. His hands loosened from her shoulders. "Think we could go back to camp now? I'm freezing, and I dropped the thermos overboard." His face was damp with perspiration, which grew cold on his skin.

"He knows I know he's out here working my lease. Perhaps he won't try it again. Seventy yards," she lamented woefully. "Those pellets prob'ly didn't do any more damage than a bee sting."

"That guy knows he didn't run into any beehive," Cooper observed dryly, and retrieving his push pole, aimed the pirogue toward home. *Good crying damn,* he thought. His heart was racing so badly it would probably beat them back to camp.

9

PATCH BLAMED it on the pungent smell of raw leather and tallow scraped from hides, how it hurt to breathe in the skinning shed. It had been four days and a hundred nights since she'd announced she'd have no more sex because Cooper wouldn't declare. Oh, how she longed to repeal those words and asked over and over again in her mind what she was going to do now.

Skin nutria, that's what, she told herself, and her knife flew, snipping the hide at the webbed feet, the teeth, along the flanks, and pulling the hide from the carcass that she then tossed into a tub for Cooper to scrape. Yet despite her resolve, her mind worked as swiftly as her hands. For four days they had been, and were even this minute, playing games; pretending that they had not been to bed together, pretending that the word love had not been mentioned, pretending that each slept wonderfully sound, not dreaming of the other. It was awful!

Electricity not having been extended to the outbuildings, the shed was illuminated by two old-fashioned kerosene lanterns that cast circles of light and warmth on the worktables, leaving shadowy the rough planked floors and wooden niches holding moldboards along the walls and ceilings. Cooper worked beneath one of the circles of light. She could tell he was tired and slowing down. "You can go on up to the shack and wash up or start those samples you took today," she told him.

"I'll stick it out and wait for you, but a smoke break sounds good." He stepped away from the six-foot scraping log, which had been used for more than fifty years and had the smoothness of dark oiled teak. His arms, legs, neck and back ached. "Now I know why you don't set out more than two hundred traps," he said mournfully, massaging the small of his back.

"I told you trapping wasn't for the fainthearted."

"What's the tally so far?"

"Two hundred eighty, mostly nutria." There was more than a suggestion of worry on Patch's face. "It ought to be more. I'll get even with that poacher for stealing one whole day's trapping from me. You just wait and see. Rosalina's depending on me. So are *maman* and *grand-mère*."

"Nearly three hundred pelts is damned good, I'd say." He leaned against the skinning table and rummaged for a cigarette.

"Not considering how many four-dollar pelts you turned into twenty cents," Patch teased. He hadn't cut a pelt in two days now.

Cooper winced. It had looked so easy when Patch had demonstrated the scraping technique, but somehow the first few times he'd tried it, the fat scraper had gone clean through the pelt to the scraping log. "When are you taking them to the fur buyer?"

Her throat constricted. "When I have close to five hundred, give or take a dozen. Two more days, prob'ly, if the poachers stay away." She couldn't make herself look his way. "Are you so anxious to leave, then?"

He deflected the question. "Did you do all this by yourself last year?"

"I didn't set the first trap last year. We got as far as heating the oil, that's all. After...Rosalina's accident, I just couldn't. I fished instead, but fishing isn't

as good this winter as last. It's too cold." She took
the broom and began sweeping up bits and pieces of
tallow that had fallen from the scraper.

Cooper tilted his head at her, the smoke curling
around his face. "Tell me more about Rosalina," he
said softly.

Patch stopped sweeping, leaned her chin atop the
broom handle and sighed. Searching around for top-
ics other than sex and love was part of the pretending. Still, no one had ever paid her as much attention
as Cooper was and he did seem interested in her
answers. She was finding it easier and easier to say
to him what was in her heart. "She's different from
me, always gay and laughing. She's two years younger, taller, fairer...." Patch closed her eyes for an
instant. "*Maman*'s favorite—everybody's favorite,
really. Sometimes when I think on Rosalina I get this
bottomless fright that I'll make too little, too late, for
her...for me."

"Your mother's hard on you, isn't she? I couldn't
help but notice that first night."

Patch thought talking of mothers was dangerous.
She hesitated, then answered. "*Maman* doesn't mean
to be. It's just...she hasn't been the same since papa
died. You noticed her leg, no? She was crippled by
polio when she was a girl, but while papa was alive,
you never noticed. She danced, sang, even came out
here to camp and helped papa and me until after
Christmas. Now, her leg is a burden to her. It's all she
can manage to take the bus once a month to Baton
Rouge to see Rosalina."

The broom was in motion again.

"You can't keep up with all this by yourself. You'll
have to hire some help when I'm gone."

She gave him a long, silent look. Her heart had
spent most of the past four days knocking like it was
outside her body. Standing there in the warm skin-

ning shed, with the smell of raw leather and kerosene in her nostrils, she wondered how she could be
so calm—how she could just stand there with the
broom in her hand and Cooper before her, and not
be afraid of his leaving.

It was because she was tough, she thought, like
the furs stretched on moldboards that hung from the
ceiling, spilling the scent of dripping tallow into the
air. If he didn't declare his love, then she'd just have
to go on alone. She didn't like it, but she'd do it.
However, if there was a way to get him into her bed
again, he wouldn't leave—she just knew he wouldn't.
Most prob'ly, if she set her mind to it, she could find
something to say to lead him up to it.

"I can't afford hired help this year. Hand me that
dustpan, please."

Cooper passed over the dustpan. "Mules don't
have anything on you," he muttered.

After she'd measured out the fuel for the drying
heater, she turned down the wicks in the lanterns
and they ran through the cold winter night together,
not quite hand in hand but close enough that their
arms grazed. Cooper didn't seem to notice.

"You can bathe while I cook, no?" she said, taking
a huge slab of bacon from the refrigerator. She
lighted all four burners on the stove to chase off the
chill and put the kettle on one to boil. On another
she put a thick iron skillet, dropping bacon into it
with a splat.

She did her best to keep her eyes away from
Cooper's rugged muscular body as he slopped and
splashed and slung soap bubbles so that she had to
put lids on all the cooking pots or see supper ruined.
These past days when she had bathed, he'd lain on
his bunk with his face to the wall.

"I'm famished," he exclaimed when they finally
sat to table.

Patch picked at her plate. "I am, too, but for more than food."

His head jerked up.

She met his eyes directly. "Thinking of you is keeping me awake nights. Prob'ly we ought to talk about it, so I can get some sleep."

"We went too fast," he said evenly. "Probably because we were thrown together here in the lonely reaches of the swamp with no one else to talk—"

"That's not it, *m'sieu.*"

He was learning her moods, her ways, the intricate little patterns of life that make up an individual personality. She called him *m'sieu* now when she was shaken or unsure of her ground, unconsciously revealing her fragility. *Tread softly*, he ordered himself, studying her until the silence was piercing. "Will you come to Washington with me?"

Patch sat in her chair as if she had been there forever, as if she would never move again. "No, *m'sieu*, my life is here."

"My life, and the core of my work, is in Washington. You would have me give it all up to gallivant about...about this wilderness where you can't find more than a single human being every three miles? And then, likely as not, you'd shoot him."

She ignored the danger signals flashing in his eyes. "But if the person you want most is one of those people?"

"Have I said that?" he queried harshly.

"You could get a government job here, if that's what you want," she said almost inaudibly, saying goodbye to the dream of a partner, a lifemate, pushing the present into the future, not liking what she saw but reminding herself that she was tough.

"I could, but that's not what you need, is it?"

Every part of her went rigid with control. "I want a man to share my life."

"You want a man to surrender." He spoke with a
savage intensity. "You want a man to take on your
identity." His voice dropped to a cruel whisper. "I
haven't had much luck with women, beginning
with my mother, so don't ask me for something I
can't give."

"You fault your mother for leaving you, and because of that, fault all women. I wouldn't abandon
you like she did."

Cooper went white about his lips. "You think you
have the right to pass judgment on my mother?"

She studied the scraps of food on her plate, then
raised her eyes to his. "No more than you judge me
by her, *m'sieu.*"

He slammed his fist down on the table. "Stop
calling me *m'sieu!*"

She sat there across from him, saying nothing for
the longest time. Finally she spoke. "I understand
now. You must have this hate for your mother. It's
what keeps her alive for you! But neither will *I*
surrender... *Cooper.* I know there isn't much to me
flesh- and bone-wise, but what there is, you taught
to burn with passion, to glory in desire so that all I
am throbs with delight when you touch me. I am of
a practical nature, too—that's the Cajun in me. We
Cajun's make do. I'll make do without you, if I have
to, I'm tough!"

She got up from the table and went to her bunk.

"You're making a mountain out of a molehill."

"There are no mountains here."

"You're so right. It's all mud and I'm drowning in
it! Stop crucifying me!" he shouted. "All that's happened between us is a little sex—"

She gave him a caustic smile. "Nice boys don't
talk about sex."

"You're lovely, really lovely," he snarled.

Patch gave no response while she removed one

boot, then the other, and lay down, pulling the quilts up to her neck. "I was teasing you when I said you were a bit small in the thighs, but I'm not when I say you're small between the ears! Pleasant dreams!" With a definite flounce she tugged the quilts over her head.

Cooper couldn't give in so easily. It wasn't in his makeup. "The silent treatment again. It won't work this time," he said witheringly. "I know all your little tricks now." He sat at the table, massaging his aching fingers, glancing at her bunk now and again, though all that was visible was a stray curl. He felt drawn to her despite himself. Because it seemed the fitting thing to do, he stomped over to her and jerked the blankets from her head. "You're going to sleep all night in your clothes?"

The caustic smile reappeared. "Would you like to undress me?"

His eyes ignited. "Gaston has you pegged to the penny," he said gutturally. "He called you a courtesan. He was right."

"That mountain you spoke of is the hate you hold for your mother, Cooper. It has blinded you to finding happiness, with me or any other woman." She raised up on her elbows, the shining depths of her black eyes fathomless. "We are all flawed. Loving is forgiving those flaws. I forgive you yours. You ought to forgive your *maman* hers."

Cooper rocked back on his heels. He was overcome with an urge to get away—from the swamp, from Patch, before both swallowed him up. He had never before been stuck in a small shack with a woman who grated on his nerves, who harassed him like this. Or a woman so real in his dreams he could taste her, touch her, smell the vision of her. He clenched his jaw when she began to take off her outer garments and toss them to the foot of her bunk. When she reached her underwear he could see her breasts swelling beneath the tightly stretched cotton. "Stop flaunting yourself!" he insisted unreasonably.

"Turn your eyes to the wall!" she shouted in return.

Cooper went to the table to sit down and recover. Time passed. All around him was the silence of the swamp, broken only by the ticking of the old clock on the stove; that in itself was sufficient to get on his nerves, and he stiffened obstinately.

"You're all wrong for me," he said aloud. "Wrong, wrong! Double wrong!" But Patch didn't hear him. Weary beyond belief, she was already asleep. He stubbed out his cigarette in the ceramic ashtray Patch had made in the fourth grade. Then he ran his finger around its chipped edges...round and round while old dead flecks of his past hurts spiraled inward as a tornado might have twirled them. Oh, good creeping damn! He was no good at love or loving.

He could only think of escape.

PATCH CAME PARTLY AWAKE in that strange ambience between consciousness and unconsciousness. She opened her eyes, but there was only darkness and cold; a cold so intense that it was almost tactile. It drove her shivering from her bunk. She turned on the stove, oven and top burners, and that gave her enough light to see that Cooper had stacked the dinner dishes in the sink and that the old clock said four.

She heard the rasping sound of a striking match and turned, seeing it flare, and Cooper's face illuminated for an instant.

"It's colder than charity," she said. "I've never seen it this cold, not even in February. Wish I'd brought the radio for weather reports."

The tip of his cigarette blazed as Cooper inhaled. The smoke trailed across the window, caught by a faint sliver of moonlight. When he remained silent, Patch shrugged, and set to making coffee. The spout from the rain barrel was frozen. Her shoulders sagged. "Have to use bayou water for coffee," she said, dipping it out of the bucket under the sink. It, too, had a thin crust of ice.

Cooper watched her, devouring her with his eyes, then his tongue just picked up and made words by itself. "Come over here and let me hold you."

Patch stood with her arms unmoving against her sides, experiencing bewildering eruptions of joy. *Cooper—you're sure?* He couldn't have heard that, she thought. It had only been a question in her brain. But he must've read her mind. People in love could. He was answering, naked need evident in his voice.

"I don't know what I'm sure of anymore, except that I need you." Once more, he told himself, and then he had to leave, before the desolate swamp surrounding him began to look like the Promised Land, or Patch, in some mysterious way, managed to capture his total being. He dropped his cigarette in the tin can by his bed.

"Is this just sex again?"

"Do you have to be furnished an explanation for everything? I want you. I've been aroused all night just thinking of you, remembering the way you feel lying next to me."

Patch was thrilled. It was terrible the way her brain said no, and her body screamed yes. "I love it when you talk like that, Cooper. Say some more."

"Talking isn't what I have in mind. And don't you get started. Just come over here."

"You'll remember that I said we wouldn't do it again until you declared."

"I declare that I need you desperately," he said in a husky whisper.

She closed her eyes and sighed. That wasn't the declaration she had in mind, but then her breasts were humming with anticipation and there was this great warmth filling her secret places. Cooper was all confused about how true love went anyway; he wasn't a man who understood destiny. A woman had to make allowances. She gathered the quilts from her bunk, piling them on his, and as Cooper took her into his arms a half scowl of apprehension lined his face. She found his furrowed brow with her fingertips. "Don't worry so," she implored. "Talking isn't what I have in mind, either."

Something like a broken groan erupted from his throat as his mouth bent to hers, his tongue hot and moist, tasting the sweetness of lost sleep. His hands traveling her flesh spoke of his inarticulate longing, then he was plundering her body, his rhythm slow, controlled, holding back until Patch called out to him with rapturous delight. Then the dam not only cracked within him, but the debris of a lifetime came rushing into a valley, carrying with it the residue of torment, of anger and guilt and hurt.

Patch expelled a long shuddering breath, quivering with leftover sensations that seemed somehow to turn back like an outgoing tide that finds itself swept back to shore on an incoming wave. Spent passion rebuilding of its own accord, disregarding flesh still tender from the assault of his lips and body. She turned in Cooper's embrace languidly, letting her hand creep along his thigh. "Would it be all right if we did it again?"

"There you go," he said huffily, trying for anger and failing because he discovered to his delight that his body had its own answer. "Yes. Yes, I believe we

can," he said in earnest, and he began to touch her
with a questing tenderness.

Afterward they slept a while and awoke to a
changing of light, the saffron yellow of approaching
dawn visible in the fraction of sky that could be seen
from where they lay.

The stove had been roaring for hours and now the
room radiated heat. Patch was light-headed as she
moved from Cooper's side, dragging on his robe,
which she found on the floor beside the bunk. "I can
hear your heart beating," she said.

His elbow was thrown up over his eyes, and his
lips moved, curving into a smile. "My heart has
stopped and backed up."

"Have you ever felt this way before, Cooper?"

The smile went away. "Go make coffee," he demanded softly.

"Two times, Cooper," she exclaimed in adoration.
"And it's not even Sunday."

His elbow lifted enough that he could look into
her eyes. "I'm only thirty-three years old. Twice is
no big thing. You're not supposed to go around
counting."

"But you said—"

"Just forget what I said," he pleaded hoarsely,
dropping his elbow back over his eyes, then lifting it
again to add hollowly, "You really know how to
boost a man's ego."

"I'm glad," she said.

"Go make coffee...please," he uttered in a feeble
hiss of air.

The heat in the walls had unfrozen the rain-barrel
spigot jutting over the old sink. Patch made coffee
properly, and while they were drinking it, she tilted
her head as if to listen.

"You hear something?" Cooper asked, trying to be
nice despite the testy way he was feeling.

"A big diesel coming up the bayou." She went to
the window and looked out, eyeing the turn in the
canal a quarter mile away. After standing there some
minutes, she gave a tight squeal. "It's Gaston and his
brother, Parker, nosing this way!"

"So?"

Patch rushed to the sink, threw off Cooper's robe
and began dipping out of the old bucket, whimpering as the chill water splashed on her skin.

"For crying out loud," Cooper exclaimed at her
antics. "Just get dressed."

"They'll smell you on me." She began to drag her
fingers through her wildly disordered hair.

"You'll never be able to disguise the fact that
we've made love. You look too satisfied."

She gave him a piteous look and he changed his
mind.

"Bragging again! To me, *about me!*" she cried
incredulously, and began flying about the shack,
stopping once to pull on her pants, again for her
moccasins, her shirt, snatching her quilts off Cooper's bed to make her own so that there would be no
telltale hints for the sharp-eyed Cajun brothers.

Bacon was frying and she was standing purposefully in the door when Gaston leaped from the stern
of the boat onto the wharf. The prow was heaped
with nutria carcasses to be disposed of, evidence that
trapping on the Voisin lease was excellent this season.

Parker Voisin shambled into the shack behind his
brother. Parker always shambled, and it caught
one's attention, because he was thin and wiry with a
narrow olive-skinned face and you expected him to
move like the wind instead of a big rambling bear.
When people commented on this he laughed, saying
he didn't dare pick up his feet lest he put one down

on a little human. There were so many babies in his house he had to wade through them.

He greeted Cooper with a shy grin. "Sorry I didn't get to meet you properly the other day when I picked up Gaston, but we were running late getting to camp."

"You were running late," Gaston injected slyly. "Staying behind to do who knows what with your wife."

Parker's black eyes twinkled. "One learns to savor one's woman before spending two weeks in the swamps alone, eh?"

Patch offered coffee and breakfast, which the brothers accepted with alacrity. Between mouthfuls of food, Parker talked to Patch, the discussion at first centering around the unusual cold and the coming Christmas holidays. After she'd refilled their cups, he said, "We're dumping our carcasses in alligator alley today," mentioning the local name for a bayou not on any map. "We'll take yours, too, if you want."

"I want," she said. "It'll save me a trip and a day's trapping."

Parker turned to Cooper. "Would you like to come along? Gaston tells me you're taking water and mud samples for the EPA."

Patch held her breath. Cooper was being accepted in the swamp. Parker offering his time and company was the stamp of approval for which many outsiders waited for years. Parker couldn't know how warmly indebted to him she felt at that moment.

"I'd like to go," Cooper agreed, thinking a day away from Patch would give him the distance he needed to put his confused thoughts in some practical order. Escaping for a day, he thought resolutely, would prepare her for the more permanent parting that had to come soon. Or maybe it was to prepare

himself. He shoved that idea to the outer reaches of
his brain. Looking at her, feeling himself missing her
already, he muttered a silent oath.

"What must I do in exchange for this favor,"
asked Patch, knowing that reciprocation would be
desired, though not demanded.

"Supper!" Gaston said quickly. "We'll bring it,
you cook it." He fingered his lip, sighing unhappily.
"I'm so tired of Parker's cooking. When Rosalina
comes home...." He trailed off.

"There will be babies and more babies, and she
still won't be able to join us at camp," Parker said,
laughing. "Who will be the laggard, then, eh?"

"Agreed," said Patch, joining in Parker's laughter.
"I'll get the wheelbarrow and start hauling carcasses
to the whàrf."

THE DAY FOR PATCH, working her traps alone, was a
long and weary one, made more so by the question
of Cooper's that kept pounding in her mind: *Will
you go to Washington with me?*

She dreaded the import of that question, and the
dread made the blood in her veins run as cold as the
chill wind snapping at her as it tried to find passage
beneath the warm layers of clothing she wore.

She would shrivel up and die in a city. And Washington! All those squat gray buildings and gold
domes housing politicians—the bane of the swamp.
Making decisions that affected her livelihood, creating a sportsman's paradise out of her wilderness,
one that God had not yet finished. For the Atchafalaya Basin was still shifting its mud and quicksand
and rich silt, and the Mississippi River had on more
than one occasion tried to move its path into the
basin. Would do it, too, prob'ly, a million years from
now, despite politicians and bridges and dams and
the Corps of Engineers that so assiduously charted
its every moving inch.

A siege of herons, startled into flight by her approach, soared as one on outspanned wings, guided by innate compasses to another part of the swamp. Shading her eyes with a hand, Patch watched the flock out of sight, her gaze drifting over the landscape—winter gray, alien, inhospitable to man unless that man or woman knew its secrets as she did.

Yet, come spring the swamp would be a riot of color: yellow honeysuckle and dandelions, lavender hyacinths, the fluttering orange wings of monarch butterflies—alluring and luring. And then humans had better beware, had better have certain knowledge of the dangers that lurked there. Beneath the surface of gray-black water were prehistoric-looking alligators, and above were wolves, coyotes, diamond-backed water snakes camouflaged in the subtle green shadows cast by pine and oak and cypress. And in the summer a sun beamed down like a benediction on fishnets and crawfish traps while the swamp dwellers cursed and swatted at ever-present swarms of mosquitos and gnats. The swamp, with its winter trapping, summer fishing, autumn hunting was her home. She wanted Cooper alongside her for these changing seasons.

Patch sighed, and her breath misted before her eyes. A sense of sadness surged up within her. This was where she belonged. She would never leave, so if Cooper didn't stay, he would be lost to her forever. She wasn't sorry now that she'd bedded with him again. It wasn't like she had gone back on her word to anyone; not to Rosalina, not to God—only herself. She took up her mud pole and pushed the heavily laden skiff past a slick of mud as thick as cold pudding. Nutria were stacked up to the oarlocks. She felt a shiver of anticipation. She had her pelt count now.

She would sell her furs in Catahoula tomorrow.

10

WITH A START, Patch came awake and sat up in bed, regretting that she had not moved the clock nearer so that she could reach out and shut it off. She yawned and stretched, and by the time she had convinced herself to leave the warmth of her bed and go turn off the alarm, it had wound itself down with a last vibrating clack. "Time to get up, Cooper."

From his bunk he muttered something unintelligible.

"Five more minutes, then, but no more. We still have to pack our dirty laundry, take yesterday's catch off the moldboards and load up the boat."

The list in her mind kept her occupied as she dressed, doubling up on insulated underwear. It was inexplicably cold; her whole body was quaking with it, but weather was not uppermost in her mind. Yesterday the Voisin brothers and Cooper had not only dumped the nutria carcasses, they had brought back a deer, half of which she must drop off at Parker's house in Catahoula to feed his growing family. And after she sold her furs she must replenish supplies—fuel, fresh clothes, food—not forgetting something special to be cooked up for Christmas Day. And since Gaston was still insisting that he was going to see Rosalina on Christmas, she wanted to buy Rosalina a gift for him to deliver. It would be more special than having *maman* take it.

She stepped outside to switch on the generator, and reemerged with her teeth chattering. Cooper was finally stirring. He stretched and groaned.

"It's not even daylight, yet this cold is killing!"

"I told you not to sleep naked," she said, spying his bare golden-haired chest. "Dress warmly. I want to be on the canal the instant there's light." She waved her hand toward the table, which was strewed with charts and the reports he had worked on until far into the night. "You'd better get all this stuff ready to mail, or see it left behind."

"I'd forgotten how bossy you can be," he rasped with dour amusement, pulling blankets up to his chin.

"I have lots of business to take care of today, and I want enough time at home to take a long soak in the tub and shampoo my hair. You may not appreciate the little things in life, but I do."

"Come over here and let me show you what I appreciate."

It took a second for her to shift mental processes, to register the seductive quality in his voice. "What you're thinking about makes you sleepy afterward, so even if we had time for the one, we wouldn't for the other. Get up."

"The man who marries you is really going to be in for it," he replied with some asperity, but dragging bedclothes with him, he threw his legs over the side of the bunk.

"I expect the man who marries me will get used to it," was her soft reply.

"No doubt," he said dryly.

"I'll be outside loading the boat. Coffee's dripping. It'll be ready in a minute."

By the time he had dressed, had had his coffee and was packing his duffel, Patch reentered the shack, rubbing her arms against the chill. "You don't have to take the duffel, just your dirty clothes for *maman* to wash."

"I'm taking everything."

An indefinable dread came over Patch, a chill burrowing beneath the surface like some small enraged animal. First it flowed slowly, like the mists coming up on a warm night; then it surged and gained in strength so that her heart began to beat with double force. "You're not coming back," she accused in a hoarse whisper.

He stopped packing, turning to her. Beard shadow did not hide the ruthlessly determined set of his jaw. His eyes were somber, submerging a truth he was not yet able to accept. "I told you I couldn't promise anything."

He couldn't help but see that he was hurting her, yet he was being driven by something more compelling than her pain. Anyone who had been through what he had, and had the scars to prove it, didn't go asking to get stepped on again.

"That's what you said with your brain. Your heart said...said...." She swallowed, becoming mute and dispirited, hating him the way you can hate only someone you love who has hurt you.

Remember when you asked me if I'd ever felt like this before? If it means anything, I haven't, and I can't imagine ever feeling like this again."

"That doesn't make me feel good now." If only the motor won't start in the boat, she thought, then she'd have an excuse to delay the trip.

"Ten days ago we hadn't even met," he continued, as if she could make sense of it when he could not. She was looking into him, Cooper thought, seeing with those wide dark eyes of hers all of the depths to which he had stooped, staggered or fallen.

"Ten days ago was another life," she answered, paralyzed a moment, unable to shift her feet. "You're walking away from fate."

Her eyes traveled from his feet to the top of his head, indelibly etching his image on her brain forever. Her pride was as great as his stubbornness.

She could neither beg him to stay nor plead with him to love her. She made a tiny gesture of dismissal, as though all that had passed between them had been swept behind like a fragile shadow cast away from substance.

"Patch—don't hate me for this."

Her soft laughter chilled him to the bone. "But I do hate you, *m'sieu*. Loving you is the difficult part."

He saw the burning frustration written in her look—the frustration that she was being deprived of something she wanted, thwarted by the person who had the power of giving. His heart ached suddenly, a brief flare-up of the old pain. Not now, he thought. He wouldn't give in to it now. "Look, I'm sorry, but I've just come to the end of myself."

"You're a stubborn man, Cooper. A thirsty man doesn't turn away from an oasis. You heard *grand-mère*; she said our fortunes never change. What's written is written. I'll go warm up the boat motor and then I must batten down the camp. We leave in fifteen minutes." She moved toward the door, her spine straight, passing Cooper without a glance. She opened the door and went out into the cold.

Cooper went back to his packing, rationalizing to himself that he had won. He felt something go numb inside; it was an empty triumph.

DETERMINED TO DEMONSTRATE her indifference to his leave-taking, Patch when talking was necessary spoke to Cooper casually, allowing no hint of passion or pain to pass her lips, allowing no telltale gleam in her eyes.

The nutria furs, stacked neatly into old coffee-bean sacks bought for fifty cents apiece off the docks in New Orleans, were piled one atop the other in the boat, deflecting some of the wind that cut through their layers of clothing like an ice sword. When they reached the old pier in front of the house on the levee, Patch accepted Cooper's offer to help exchange the empty fuel drums for full ones and unload the furs into her pickup. Every minute with him now was precious, delaying his going.

"If it's all right with your mother, I think I'll bathe. I don't want to get on the road looking like this," Cooper said once the last sack of furs was wedged tightly into the bed of the truck.

"I'm sure she won't mind, and *grand-mère* will feed you lunch."

"A bath is enough." His gaze began to wander over her, but he jerked it back.

Natalie was taking a nap, but they found Grandmère Duval puttering about the kitchen. Patch gave her a hug. "I missed you, *grand-mère*, especially your cooking. Wish I could talk you into coming back to camp with me."

The old woman inspected her granddaughter. "You look worried, no? What's gone wrong?"

"We had poachers, but I think I nicked one and he hasn't been back. Trapping is good. I've enough pelts to pay the deposit on Rosalina's operation, and—"

"What about your man?" said Grand-mère Duval slyly, eyeing the bathroom door.

Patch felt her face going warm. "He's finished his work and is leaving. When he gets out of the shower, he'll be wanting to collect his car keys."

"He'll be coming back, no?"

Suddenly Patch did not want to be in the kitchen when Cooper emerged from his bath. She felt hot tears threatening to trickle down her cheeks. "I have errands to run if I'm to make it back to camp before dark, *grand-mère*. Tell *maman* I'll see her when I get back from town."

At the fur buyer's all the talk was of the weather.

A front over the Pacific coast was holding back warm air, allowing arctic winds to swoop down into the lower states. The entire country was suffering from unprecedented blizzards, ice storms and sub-freezing temperatures. When Patch heard about the ice and snow debilitating two-thirds of the nation, she thought herself lucky and stopped complaining. Clear, starlit nights set animals stirring, right into her traps.

She got just over two thousand dollars for her pelts, and as the cash was counted out into her hand, she began to tremble.

"Don't that government man you got out to your camp get a third of this, Patch?" Mr. Dominick asked teasingly, as he put the last ten-dollar bill into her palm.

Patch stiffened. "He paid *me* for the privilege, and you mind your own business, Dom."

"Lor! Got a temper just like your pa had, you do," he said, laughing. "You bring that government man around next time. I want to see how much Cajun you worked into 'im." The trappers waiting in line to sell their pelts laughed. Ignoring them Patch gathered up the coffee-bean sacks.

One of the old-timers followed her out to her truck. A hand-rolled cigarette dangled from his thin mouth. "Got time to pass?" he asked.

"A few minutes, Remy, what's on your mind?"

He struck a kitchen match with the flick of a ragged fingernail, putting flame to his cigarette. The extra paper at the end flared. "You seen any coy-dogs out your way?"

Patch's interest rose. Twenty or thirty years ago some dogs had gotten loose in the swamp, mating with wolves. Their progeny in turn had mated with coyotes. For lack of a better name the trappers called the vicious animals coy-dogs. As a rule they were human shy, but they stole out of traps and could cut into profits. "No, I haven't. Why?"

"A trapper from over to Bayou Sorrel come on a pack taking a deer. When they saw him they kept on feeding. Something peculiar going on in the swamp this season what with this cold stirring animals to ground." He cleared his old man's throat and spat. "You know your pa and me went back a long ways. We trapped together afore he even married Natalie. You got any problems out to your camp, you send word, I'll come."

It was the virtue of old men to mistrust and be cautious, and Patch was warmed by the old trapper's caring. "Thanks, Remy, I'll do that. The Voisin brothers have been looking in on me though, so you don't have to worry. And Bayou Sorrell's on the opposite side of the basin. Doubt if I'll have any trouble with coy-dogs."

"You'll keep an eye out just the same, no?"

"You can count on it, Remy."

He opened his mouth to say something more, and fearing he was going to ask about Cooper, Patch swung into her truck. "I've got to get going, Remy. In case I don't see you before, Merry Christmas."

He touched his fingers to his hat. "Merry Christmas to you, too. Mention me to Natalie."

"I will." With a last wave she was off on the remainder of her errands. She hurried through them, feeling apprehensive for no discernible reason, knowing only that she wanted to return home. She got a box of candy for *grand-mère*—chewy ones with nuts, for the old woman didn't hold with creams and soft centers. Those were for old folks with no teeth of their own. She found a green woolen sweater for *maman*, for green was her favorite color. Patch herself never wore green if she could help it, not since she'd heard folks didn't trust people who wore it. A superstition prob'ly, she thought, but she stayed away from it anyway, thinking it kept her integrity intact.

While buying Rosalina's gift, a compulsion for Cooper came over her. The feelings were so strong that blood drained from her face and her legs went rubbery, making the clerk who was wrapping Rosalina's sweater inquire if she was ill.

She leaned against the counter, her color high, unable to elude erotic reverie. She felt his huge hands kneading her small breasts, his lips sucking gently at the hollows in her neck, and his mouth everywhere. Oh, lor! Now she regretted not telling Cooper goodbye, regretted not crawling into bed with him that morning.

"Ma'am?"

Patch gazed at the clerk with unseeing eyes, then reality penetrated. "Oh. Oh, I'm sorry." She took the gaily wrapped package and fled.

At the house on the levee Natalie was waiting for her, sitting primly on the sofa in front of a blazing fire. Cooper was gone. Patch's disappointment was so keen, it was several seconds before Natalie's voice broke through the barrier of her thoughts.

"Did you have trouble with that man?" she was asking.

"What man, *maman?*"

"What man? Cooper Vachec. He left, barely paid his respects. Did you give him the sharp edge of your tongue?"

Patch cordoned off that part of her brain that held Cooper dear. "He paid you, didn't he?"

"Don't be sassy with me," Natalie warned.

"I'm not being sassy, *maman.* He got his work done and he left, that's all." She gave her mother the money she had received from selling the furs.

"It's all there except what I needed for supplies."

She started to mention Gaston going to see Rosalina, of the gift she had purchased, but bit the words back. Natalie wouldn't approve, might even convince Rosalina not to let Gaston see her, might even warn the hospital not to let Gaston in. Oh, and she wanted Rosalina home so badly. "I have to get cleaned up now, *maman.*"

The bathroom was redolent with the fragrance of Cooper's after-shave. Lying in the tub, Patch closed her eyes, her breath catching in her throat while erotic memories took shape behind her lids. She ached to touch him, to have him touch her, longing for that feeling that made her seem to be spinning through the heavens. Then she opened her eyes and reality overtook her. Cooper was gone. Strange that her heart should keep on beating when it felt so shattered.

With leaden arms she shampooed her hair, luxuriating in its squeaky cleanliness. She filed her nails to rid them of ragged edges and saturated her face and hands with an emollient against the elements. All for nought because there was no man to feel the softness of her skin, she told herself, but did it anyway.

Leaving the steamy bathroom, she took a towel and sat by the fire in the living room to dry her hair. Cheered by the cash Patch had given her, Natalie was in the kitchen, jointing the haunch of deer Parker had told Patch to keep for herself. *Grand-mère* was dozing in her rocking chair, and Patch gazed at her, not sighing, but wanting to. It hadn't used to be this way on sale day. When papa had sold furs they would go out to dinner, get presents, laugh. Her sigh came and she stared into the fire. She didn't think she would ever laugh again.

"Your man said to tell you he would write."

Patch jerked her gaze from the mesmerizing flames. "What good is a letter?"

The tears she had withheld began to flow, and in a low voice that did not carry to the kitchen, she confessed her love for Cooper to her grandmother, telling all that she knew about him, about his mother, his lack of trust, concealing only the fact that they had made love.

The old woman listened, rocking steadily in her chair.

"He's never coming back," Patch ended. "And I hurt so. I thought I could rid him of his hate."

"He suffers from self-deception," *grand-mère* said. "He must hate his mother. If he admitted that he loved her, it would make the pain he feels greater than what he bears now. In ways, your Cooper is no different than me. I pretend Duval is coming home when I miss him most, though I know he never will. His bones lie in a faraway land. I dress for him and I cook for him, and that eases the ache. One pretends. It makes life acceptable." She leaned forward suddenly. "You're certain this man is taken with you, no?"

"He said he was."

"Get me my trunk," *grand-mère* commanded abruptly.

Patch gaped. "Your little trunk? The one—" She had never been allowed to touch it, to peer into it, to examine its contents.

"Don't dawdle," *grand-mère* ordered. "You've wanted to know its secrets for years. Now you shall."

Patch brought the trunk from the side of *grand-mère*'s bed. A wooden portmanteau with a curved lid, its brass clasps and tooling worn thin and the wood pitted as though by sea worms. Patch placed it before her grandmother, who pulled a small brass key from her bosom and inserted it into the lock. With a grand gesture she threw back the lid.

Patch stared into the trunk, speechless, though she was seldom at a loss for words with her grandmother. "Why, there's nothing in there. I imagined your jewels, your wedding dress, old pictures, something of the first Angelicque."

"Look again," the old woman said sternly.

Patch thought perhaps *grand-mère* was off in that other world she visited so often. "It's still empty," she said quietly.

Grand-mère Duval displayed her strong white teeth. "It held a change of clothes once, for the first Angelicque, your namesake and mine. She made a good marriage. But now it's filled with hope, with dreams and desires." She reached into the trunk with a gnarled hand, stirring the musty air symbolically. "Now it's empty. I remove my hopes, my dreams to make room for yours. Take the trunk. Store up your good hopes."

"But this has been your proudest possession—" protested Patch.

"Bah! What use does a shriveled up old woman like myself have for a trunk full of dreams." She sank back in her chair, closing her hooded eyes, the wrinkled lids falling upon her once fine cheeks. "The wings come closer day by day," she muttered.

She was slipping into that other world. Patch tried to draw her back. "*Grand-mère*, what about Rosalina? She has always admired this trunk, hoping that it would be hers one day."

The wrinkled lids lifted momentarily. "Rosalina has her own rewards." Her voice was sad. She nudged the trunk with her slippered foot. "It can hold your failures, too, if you care to lug them around. I never did." For an instant her deeply lined face was devoid of expression, stark and vulnerable.

Patch was moved. "What did you ever fail at, *grand-mère*?"

"Take the trunk and go," the old woman admonished, brushing Patch aside like she would a worrisome fly. "You're keeping me from my prayers."

"Thank you for the trunk, *grand-mère*. I'll take good care of it, but it won't bring Cooper back."

"Just put the wish inside and close the lid on it. You'll see...." Her chin dropped onto her shrunken chest, her toes curled into the rug, activating the rocker, and she left Patch for another look at the great white bird.

Patch bent to kiss the dry papery cheeks. "Look under my bed Christmas Eve," she whispered.

The hooded lids raised half-mast. "Chewy centers, yes?"

An air of unwitting dismay washed over Patch. "*Grand-mère*, you've already peeked!"

"Have not..." she said, trailing off, letting her lids fall as she invoked the ghost of Duval.

Patch loaded the old trunk into the boat, handling it reverently. For good luck. For an answer. She told herself she had made her wish to appease her grandmother.

And despite the need to be on her way, she kept finding excuses not to leave the pier. Another minute to gather up spices from the kitchen; five minutes to remind her mother about a message for Rosalina or a trip to her room for spare blankets. All the while she kept an eye out for traffic on the levee road—of which there was none.

Finally, hunkered down beneath an old quilt to help deflect the wind, she threw off the stern ropes, started the motor and glanced back once at the house to see Natalie waving a handkerchief frantically in the window. All that useless trotting to and fro, Patch thought, and still she had forgotten something.

A shadow in the dogtrot caught her eye, and Cooper emerged into the sun and wind, walking down the slanting pier, hollow shadows of weariness under his eyes. His right hand gripped the duffel sling as though it held all that was dear to him.

Patch stood up in the stern, the quilt falling away, for now she wasn't aware of the cold. A joyous warmth radiated within her, throughout her torso to the tips of every limb, and the boat drifted away from the pier into the current. A stately black-and-white skimmer slit the water in the boat's wake with its long lower mandible, and Patch's gaze involuntarily swung from Cooper to the bird. Instinct registered the fact that the boat, with no hand on the tiller, was finding its own way.

Oh please, don't let me say anything silly, Patch thought as she brought the boat around in a wide circle and eased back to the pier.

Cooper nodded slightly in greeting. "I'm insane, I was halfway to New Orleans...." He shook his head, not believing his own behavior, speaking words as though they were rushing through him from a disembodied dream. "I felt all this emptiness so I turned around. I found myself missing you...." He stepped into the boat, found a dry spot for his duffel and, as the boat rocked, moved to take a seat opposite her. "I'm still not promising anything."

Then he threw up his fleece-lined collar and hunched down into his coat, studying Patch in an oddly calculating way. "Let me know when you want a rest. I'll take the tiller."

"I missed you, too," Patch replied simply, and besieged by wondrous emotions, faced into the dismal cold.

11

IT WAS ALMOST DARK when Patch turned the boat into the canal on which the camp was located. The swamp was hushed, its myriad voices sibilant except for an owl that filled the night with questions. Prow and stern lights beamed onto Stygian water, illuminating jutting stumps and the swaying moss that draped trees along the banks. Guiding the boat, adjusting speed, avoiding stumps was familiar ritual requiring no thought. Her mind was on Cooper. Whenever the opportunity presented itself she regarded him speculatively, hoping for a word or gesture that would define their relationship. But he had kept his head bent against the wind, remaining silent, and she knew he was still at war with himself.

The instant she cut the motor he was on his feet, leaping to the wharf to secure the boat. "Ten more minutes and I would've been frozen solid."

"They said in town its going to get worse," Patch replied evenly, thrilled that he was making conversation. "You might be sorry you came back."

"I don't think so. Anyway, that bridge has been crossed, hasn't it?" He was thinking of the terror he had felt that she would have been gone by the time he returned to the house on the levee. "Why don't you get the stove going inside the camp? I'll start unloading supplies."

At first she started to refuse, wanting to just be near him, then realized that was foolish what with supper still needing to be cooked, beds to be made up with fresh linens and supplies put away.

There was a thin line of perspiration on his upper lip by the time Cooper entered the shack with the last load of groceries. Patch dived into them to find the steaks and discovered they were frozen. "They weren't frozen when I bought them," she said, dismayed.

"Cook them anyway. I haven't eaten all day," Cooper admonished.

"Did you do your laundry?" He answered no and she wrinkled her nose. "I'll have to rig up a drying line in the shed. You at least have to have clean underwear."

He did not take his gaze off her as he put his duffel against the wall. "I at least have to have you. You want to know something funny? The more I have of you, the more I want." In his eyes was a great wonder, as of one who finally sees the fulfillment of a dream.

Her heart was singing. "Could we wait until after supper?"

"I didn't mean just sexually."

"Oh." She looked at him and then away, mortified.

He grinned, understanding a little of what she felt. "After supper will do nicely."

For the next hour and a half Patch didn't seem to know what to do with her hands or her eyes. When she wasn't looking, plates leaped from her fingers, frying pans slid off burners, she steeped the coffee twice.

"Maybe a little music..." Cooper said, noting her anxiety. Taking the radio she had unpacked, he plugged it into the socket over the light bulb, twirling the dials until he found a station out of Lafayette that was free from static.

Patch didn't know whether to be resentful at Cooper's attitude. She felt as though they were two people working up to reconciliation after years apart. But the soft Cajun music against the primitive activity in her body went far to soothe her jangled nerves.

"Mr. Dominick was giving away thermometers this year instead of calendars. You can tack it to the rain barrel if you want. It'll give us some idea of the temperature drop tonight. Hammer's in the shed."

"Sending me out into the cold won't cool me off much or for very long," Cooper told her, his blond eyebrows rising in slight amusement.

"Nobody's trying to cool you off. It just came to mind, that's all."

"Mr. Dominick is the fur buyer, I take it. How'd you do?"

Thoughts of being in bed with Cooper were still thronging in her mind. She could hardly contain her happiness and had to express it. His question loosened her tongue. She told of her good luck with the furs, that Mr. Dominick had asked to see him and about the chat with old Remy. One thing led to another and they were soon finished with supper, the table cleared and dishes done. With the ashtray in his hand, Cooper strolled over to the sofa and sat down.

"Is it warm enough in here now, do you think?" he asked.

Patch hung the dish towel on the antler over the sink and turned to look at him, puzzled. "Warm enough for what?"

"Warm enough for you to undress so I can watch," he said softly, his eyes clinging to the sweet curve of her neck.

She felt a fluttering of gossamer wings inside her. "We ought to turn the generator off first," she said, suddenly bashful.

He shook his head slowly. There was a calmness in his eyes that had not been there before, and a strength and knowledge about him that told of an inner battle fought and won. "You're mine. I want to see you. You don't have to be fancy about it."

Time seemed to stop as Patch made her way hesitantly across the room to stand before him. "You haven't even kissed me yet." He hardly heard the words, so soft and slurring was her voice. Her face suffused with color, and her hands trembled on the buttons of her flannel shirt.

"I will," he promised hoarsely. "And plenty more besides." His eyes remained on her for quite some time before he said, "You told me you loved me and I'm trying to imagine why."

She knew that she must respond, knew that her answer was terribly important to him—to herself. "I like the way you do things; your courtesy to others. I like the way you make me feel inside, like I'll never be cold or lonely again." Her voice dropped. "I like the way you lose yourself in me...."

He moved then, very quickly, scooping her slight body into his arms and carrying her to his bunk, where he tucked her between the cool clean sheets. "I'll go turn off the generator now," he said thickly, and Patch knew that she had said all the right and true things.

WHEN COOPER AWOKE he was sore in the back, hungry and happy. Patch was frying bacon, and there was a faint glimmer of light outside, so he knew it was day. Cold and gray, but leaden weather couldn't lessen his feeling of well-being.

For a time he lay staring at the ceiling, thinking of the night before. He felt all clean and new inside. Whatever love was, he knew he had it, and badly, like a disease with no cure. He was primed and ripe for it after the hard lonely years. He couldn't for the life of him figure out why he had fought against it or what had made him leave.

Every mile he had retraced yesterday had been bringing him back to Patch—a sprite, a swamp rat, a woman who was different from any he had ever known, but not so different from himself in her heart. She had a way of saying things that pinched his ego, but that would change. Before last night he had known every nook and cranny of her body, known the way her soft velvety flesh felt against the rougher texture of his own, yet that had not taken the wonder out of it. He breathed with a content- ment he had not believed possible.

Hearing Cooper stirring, Patch looked over at him and found him smiling. "Get up and earn your keep," she said with mild rebuke, guessing at his thoughts. "There's a boat to be put back in the water and traps to be run, and the rain barrel froze up again last night. If you want a wash, you'll have to haul water."

He laughed mockingly. "Yes, ma'am. So little and bossy and full of life. Aren't you just a bit testy this morning? I'd think after last night...." He was re- membering the sweet small rise of her breasts, the alluring fragrance of her body, things she had said in love; how she had moaned until he had thought he was hurting her, and when he'd stopped, how she had pleaded with him not to.

"It's peculiar to me that all of a sudden you want to rattle on about sex. What I needed last night, I didn't get." Her dark curls were in fine dishabille, her eyes glowing, the flesh beneath them faintly shadowed, which added a piquancy to her features.

"If it's sleep you crave, suppose you crawl back in bed and I'll run traps by myself today?"

Her eyes filled with a grave seriousness and something of fear. "You don't know enough. You'd get lost. I'd have to turn every trapper out just to go looking for you. Fine name that'd earn you."

"I didn't know my image counted."

"There's lots you don't know." Now that he had declared himself she was never going to let him out of her sight. "And I meant to ask. Did you mail your reports?"

"It's the only thing I did remember to do yesterday, before I got back to you."

She smiled at that and softened. "I made biscuits this morning. You'd better get up and get them while they're hot, no?"

He nearly froze in the outhouse and came back swearing. But he warmed up by swinging his arms after he'd washed up. He spent all of breakfast trying to coax Patch back to bed—with him. She gloried in his asking but was adamant in her refusal. "You figure out a way to lure those nutria into the shed to skin themselves and you can bed me," she said, laughing, pulling on her cotton work gloves.

Just as they were preparing to push the little skiff off the bulwarks Parker Voisin cruised up to the wharf out front and shambled over, flapping his thin arms for warmth to ask Patch how his family was faring, and if there was any message from his wife.

"Only that she expects you home for Christmas because it's too cold to bring the children out to camp this year. And she appreciated the deer."

A look of melancholy closed over his face. "That's all, no?"

Patch grinned. "She said to remind you that her bed is cold and empty."

"If it gets any colder out here, I'll be warming her toes sooner than she thinks." He winked at Cooper and turned to shuffle off, anxious to return to his trap line. Patch made him wait while she went to get Rosalina's gift.

"In case I'm not about camp when Gaston goes. Tell him I said 'good luck,' and tell my sister I miss her and want her home."

As THE DAYS WENT BY Patch noticed that Cooper was beginning to get the feel of the swamp and that he loved it. It was a rough life with the cold and the wet and having to live cramped in the small shack, but there was something about the smell of the earth, the vastness of the swamp beneath winter-bright stars or a sunlit saffron sky that compensated. It made tiredness and aching muscles small things compared to the love they had for each other.

The best times were when she and Cooper lay close to each other at night and talked of many things, while the wind moaned softly about the shack. It was good quiet talk. They had not come to any agreement about marriage, or even discussed it, but Cooper made plans.

"You'll have to come to Washington with me and help me clear out my apartment."

"And meet your landlady, prob'ly," she put in slyly.

He pulled her tighter in the circle of his arm. "You'll be nice to her. She's an old lady."

"You said she was beautiful!"

"She is, and eighty if she's a day."

Patch bit him on the neck.

"I have some money saved. That and my veteran's perks ought to be enough to make the down payment on a house."

"Better a shrimp boat. It'll pay for itself."

"A house. I want to put down roots like those old cypress stumps—nothing budges them. That's what I want. I'm sure I can get summer work with the

Corps of Engineers. That'll leave us free to trap during the winters."

Patch did not want to exchange her bliss for pride. When Cooper talked of marriage she had a sense of worlds colliding, of two realities coming together like airplanes on a disaster course. There was no easy way to tell him of her pledge to Rosalina, so she didn't. But she could see Rosalina lying in her arms, oil-scalded, crying, "I'm hurt, no? Oh, Patch, we'll have to put off our wedding. You'll wait, won't you? Won't you? Until I'm well?"

And when she had these thoughts her hands got damp and trembled. Cooper imagined the trembling was an answering approval and moved her hands to explore his body. The feel of his flesh voiced a deeper, wilder, fiercer message in Patch's blood, and for a time she was beyond the reach of any word or thought or sound.

Later she encouraged him to speak of his past.

"I don't like to talk about it. I lived with bitter narrow-minded people, but they had this pious way of looking for sympathy. Miss Emma was raising this poor little whelp orphaned and abandoned by his ma. But she never let me forget my mother went off with a man, and she called her a tramp. When nobody was looking I got whipped; when they were, I got a calf to raise." He chuckled bitterly. "I raised that calf spring and summer and took it to the county fair in the fall. It won first prize for me—a two-year scholarship to the University of Arkansas. I had to wait six years before I was old enough to go, but I had it to look forward to."

It had been a long time since Cooper had deliberately thought about where he had been born and how he'd been raised. A comment now and again brought back only bitterness. Sustained thoughts about it made him weak suddenly, afflicted by an odd emptiness, a vague embarrassment that he had been so impotent in his youth. He moved restlessly as if to get away from his thoughts. "All that's in the past. I want to forget it." He turned and kissed her shadowy face. "All my life I've been more or less alone. Now I have you. You're all I want."

His touch made Patch go all warm and weak. She murmured, "It's a good thing I'm lying down, or I'd fall down, prob'ly."

"Fall over my way," he whispered gutturally. "I'm hungry for you again." And he guided her hips astride his own so she could tell exactly where his hunger lay.

WEATHER REPORTS morning and night told of a nation gripped in one of the worst winters of the century. The mercury in the thermometer on the rain barrel had been below zero for three days. Patch twisted the dial for music. "All they tell us is what we know already!"

Despite the arcticlike weather, and sometimes having to skin nutria that were frozen solid by the time they got them back to camp, the pelts piled up. Patch did not intend to make another trip into Catahoula until after Christmas week. Cooper had reports ready to mail, so she had flagged trappers as they passed to and fro on the canal, spreading word for anyone going in to stop by. She hoped one would soon because Cooper was coming down with cabin fever. He needed a man to talk to.

She could pick out all the signs—he snapped at her over nothing, became frustrated about his reports and cursed the cold, over which they had no control. She did her best to ease him through it. And though she was seeing him at his worst, she was happy beyond counting. She had her man. She reached out to smooth the grim curl from his lips, and let her fingertips trail down the thick cords of his neck.

He raised his eyes from charts on the table to look at her. "I've been nasty, haven't I?"

"It happens when anyone isn't used to being in the swamp. Even the strongest sometimes feel that the sky is hugging the mud flats, crowding them out. I imagine there's any number of partners at each other's throats by now with this weather."

He caught her hand and brought it to his lips. "I want us to go into Catahoula and get married."

"Get married...." Patch stopped, her mouth open, the words trembling on her tongue. Cooper laughed at her reaction.

"What do you think I've been talking about night and day—playing checkers?" His hand moved to the open collar of her shirt, his thumb circling gently against the vein throbbing in the hollow of her neck.

She moaned inside her heart, stiffening herself against the clamor in her blood. The temptation was so great to say yes, to forget her pledge, to lie to him. But a lie could lead you anywhere, down streets you didn't want to travel, into little corners of mistrust. His mother had lied to him about coming home, had cheated him out of a happy childhood. The truth was better. He understood truth. "I can't Cooper, not yet."

As if afraid of any sudden movement he very carefully withdrew his hand and sat back. He felt as if Patch had slapped him, slapped him straight in the face. The little knot of muscle above his jaw jerked visibly. His brow was like a thundercloud. "Can't?"

She shook her head, her dark eyes huge and pleading with him to understand. "I made a promise to Rosalina." She tried to explain while he listened woodenly.

"You led me on," he rasped. "Made a fool of me

coming and going. You let me rattle on about a house, finding work...." His bewilderment gave way to a muted anger, and the anger in turn yielded to an uneasy pain. He was too close to his past now after having dredged it all up for Patch to examine. The old wounds of being unwanted, rejected, unloved felt raw and weeping again. It had been the same all his life. Every time a little happiness came his way and things started looking good, something always happened.

"I didn't lead you on. I want what you want. We just have to wait." She thought of the little trunk *grand-mère* had given her, wondering now who it was that answered those hopes and wishes.

Cooper was having none of it. His gaze flickered over her like the harsh strokes of a leather whip. "A little lesson in the facts of life—Cajun-style!" he uttered, lacing the words with grim cynicism.

"I made a vow and I have to keep it," she said, weeping. "Don't be angry—"

"Angry?" he said sarcastically. "Why should I be angry? I've been having a wonderful time. And as for the plans we had—what the hell, they weren't much anyway. We can forget all about that."

"Cooper, don't," she begged reproachfully. "Don't do this to yourself, or me. I love you."

"But not enough to marry me now." He clenched and unclenched his fists, finally slamming one down upon the table with a powerful blow.

She did not know how long she sat there—not thinking, not moving, just being—while his anger suffocated her. The striking rasp of a match heightened her consciousness, causing her to focus on him. He was lighting a cigarette.

"It wouldn't be fair for me to have such happiness...not while Rosalina languishes between rest homes and hospitals. I couldn't be so selfish. I feel

guilty enough as it is," she added hoarsely, "with us
pleasuring ourselves the way we do while Rosalina
and Gaston...."

Her voice trailed off. She was unable to state more
clearly what was in her heart, yet she wanted desperately to reassure him of her love. Her hand crept
toward his.

Her touch seared him. He studied her a long time
before he spoke. "Leave me alone," he said tone-
lessly, unable to plead his cause now in case she
thought him self-centered. He wanted to be all good
things in her eyes.

"All right, I will!" she spat, jerking her hand back,
feeling bruised, aching because she was unable to
make it right between them without breaking her
word of honor.

It was as if lines of tension flowed between them
and held and held. Patch couldn't change his attitude and finally gave up. Fortified with inner out-
rage, he treated her with matchless courtesy, making
no reference by word, gesture or innuendo to all the
intimacies and love they had shared. She was too
proud to cry, but got down on her knees each night
and prayed to St. Jude, the patron saint of hopeless
causes, first naming Cooper, then that Gaston would
be successful in coaxing Rosalina home. Afterward
she lay in her bunk feeling the sharp loss of Cooper's
warmth and encircling arms.

She refused to let him trap with her, returning
each afternoon terrified that she'd find him gone
with a trapper headed into Catahoula.

Cooper thought of leaving constantly. Yet having
decided to stay he was seized with a lassitude born
of a pride that had served him well in all those bad
years. He didn't know how to tell Patch and still
save face. He suffered, spending his days alone. The
long nights were the worst. That was when it

was hardest to keep from thinking. He pulled his thoughts away from Patch every time they strayed to her, but it did no good. He couldn't help himself. She was too close, a reality as much a part of him now as an arm or leg.

Enclosed in her own anguish during the long nights, Patch could hear him tossing and fighting with his pillow and cursing the world, until enough daylight came that she could get up and begin the morning's tasks.

THE BLACKNESS IN THE SHACK WAS ABSOLUTE. Patch came awake in a panic with a strange prickling racing up her spine. Something was wrong, out of kilter. The cold was like a gossamer net, brushing her face and hands, but that wasn't it. The ancient odor of sour mud filled with decay was strong in her nostrils and she lay very still, listening for the thousand voices of the swamp; wind soughing in willows, fish leaping, the after splash, water brushing against wharf pilings, the rustlings of insects, cotton rats, the throaty bawl of a bull alligator, the howl of a coyote. But she heard nothing.

Her mind would not accept the possibility of silence. She listened harder, unable now to locate even the sound of the big boat bumping against the wharf tires—a sound so constant she usually ignored it. Consciously she waited for the cry of a bird, the snort of a buck or the faint rustling of a ground animal to break the broody stillness, but none came.

She looked over toward Cooper's bunk. In the utter dark she could not make out even his shape beneath the mound of blankets, but sudden heightening of an inner sense told her he, too, was awake and listening. Dragging bedclothes with her, she scuttled to the stove, lighting all the burners and the oven, and warmed her hands. The stillness gave her a fear she had never experienced before, an odd sensation of doom. Even the old clock was silent. She wound the key, breaking the quiet, leaving her fingertips upon it for a moment to feel the soothing vibration of its ticking as it shot familiar sound into the vacuum.

"What are you doing up in the middle of the night?" Cooper had been aware of the silence, too, one so deep he had been listening unconsciously for something to shatter it.

She caught the broad politeness in his tone, as if he wanted to retract even that now. "It's too quiet." She went to her side of the room and began to dress. "I'm going outside to have a look."

She carried a flashlight, though she knew every inch of the bog upon which the camp stood. The damp earth was frozen. Swamp grass crunched beneath her boots, the cold and quiet engulfing her like a malevolent mantle. Nothing stirred. It was as though God had come along and scooped up all living, talking, barking, squeaking, snorting creatures.

Mist lay thick over the canals. She went to inspect the boats. At first in the glow of the flashlight she thought the tide had gone out and left the boats firmly embedded in mud. She aimed the light into the water and her breath caught, her thoughts running explosively into one another. Disbelievingly she bent down and touched the ice. And then the implication of it hit her like a physical blow. She ran back to the shack and once inside leaned against the door, her lungs heaving in an attempt to purge the icy air she had inhaled.

"Cooper," she choked. "We've got to run the traps. Now!"

He heard her, but didn't believe what he was hearing. "You're crazy. In the middle of the night? It's freezing out there."

"That's why," she gasped. "The canals are freezing." Her voice was filled with awe. "That's never happened before. We'll never get through them if we wait. We've got to get those animals out, and trip every trap so that no more are caught."

"What difference does it make?" Cooper was not uncaring, but he had been raised in the far northern corner of Arkansas where snow, ice and cold was everyday winter weather. He didn't understand the magnitude of this phenomenon in the swamp.

Patch felt tears rising in her throat. "Cooper," she said urgently. "Any animal trapped now will freeze, then rot when it warms up." She shook her head, seeing the gruesome sight in her mind's eye. "Those are pelts lost, and no creature should have to deal with man and nature at the same time. You're an environmentalist. You must understand."

"Oh, hell," he said, his thoughts black and bitter. It was useless to argue, and he knew it. If he didn't accompany her, she'd go alone.

There was a thin skim of ice on the water bucket. Patch broke it with the dipper and began to fill the coffeepot, working by the light of the gas flame on the stove. "We've got to hurry." She was breathing normally now, though her heart pounded in her chest and she was trying not to show fear. "I wonder how everyone else is faring."

"They're probably sleeping like babies," Cooper muttered dourly as he swung his legs over his bunk. He yelped as his feet hit the cold floor.

"No trapper in this basin will be sleeping through this," Patch replied solemnly.

SHE LAY OVER THE PROW of the pirogue, chopping at the ice with an ax. They were taking turns on the push pole at the stern, and despite the cold, both were sweating beneath layers of clothing. In each canal they had to hack their way to the middle where ice was only beginning to crust, then work their way back to banks wherever there was a trap. But most often they left the pirogue to walk from trap to trap on the solidly frozen bog. It was exhausting, miserably cold work even for Patch's toughened body, and outside the beam of the flashlight, cruelly dark. She and Cooper didn't talk unnecessarily, saving their strength for battling the elements. When he called to her, she stopped the swing of the ax and let her arm hang loose, grateful for the moment's respite.

"We're going to have to turn back. The ice is getting thicker." He felt the tiredness on him like a weight, pulling at his muscles, and there was a dampness in his clothes that felt chill against his skin. He didn't think Patch was faring any better.

"We can't," she groaned through the muffler wound about her lower face. Her arms ached, feeling as though they had been torn from their sockets. Little ripples of pain ran across the muscles of her chest, and each time the muffler slipped, her teeth began to chatter.

"Let's rest a minute," he ordered, pulling the push pole in over his lap. Patch stretched out in the bottom of the pirogue feeling her muscles melt and listened to the stillness. It brought a sound, one that made her stomach lurch and her throat knot. She sat up, lifting her knitted cap from her ear.

Cooper leaned forward in the gray gloom. "What is it?" He could almost smell her fear. All the feelings for her he had been holding in check, trying to deny, crowded him, making him dizzy. He grasped her wrist, and when she didn't resist, pulled her to his chest, the first time he'd touched her in days.

Her voice was a rusty whisper. "Wolves or coydogs. I can't tell which yet. They must be raiding traps."

Cooper lifted the earflap of his hat while he probed the dark with his eyes. He couldn't hear them. Patch's hearing, unconditioned to city noises, was far more keen than his own. "Which direction?"

She pointed east. "A mile, maybe less. They're howling against the wind. Oh, Cooper. Look!" She swung the light beam. "The ice is closing up behind us."

"Like hell," he said. He threw the few nutria carcasses they had harvested onto the near bank. "Maybe that'll satisfy them, if they come this way." He took up the ax. "You pole, I'll chop."

They made progress because Cooper chopped ice before the pirogue like a madman, albeit with a steady rhythm—one mile, then two. They heard the snarling and growling of the wild pack behind them, seemingly closer.

"Cooper!" Patch called. "Work to that side bank there. We're only a mile from camp as the crow flies. We can walk across the bog now that it's frozen, faster than we can cut through the ice."

Ten minutes later they stood on the shore, chests heaving. In the east a streak of light broadened into a band revealing the low banks of mist. Sweat beading on Cooper's forehead dripped to his eyebrows and began to freeze there.

"I came away without my gun," moaned Patch, picking up the stun stick. Solid as it was, it and the ax were pitiful protection against a pack of hungry wolves.

"Which way?" Cooper asked, eyeing the friendly looking mounds that were muskrats' houses. Now they looked like frozen earth forced upward by some kind of fierce subterranean disturbance.

Patch pointed with the stun stick. Cooper shouldered the ax, took Patch's hand and began to run through the mists across the icebound mud flats.

"Watch out for muskrat holes," Patch panted. A moment later she stepped into one herself, her knee slamming into the frozen mud. The fall tore her slicker, ripping it open so that cold was driven in.

The barking and growling sounds were closing in. Cooper spun about and threw down the ax. "God help us if we need that, because I can't carry it and you, too." And then he picked up the ax again, because hurtling out of the mists were a pack of coydogs.

12

AS IN A SLOW NIGHTMARE Cooper's mind separated from his body, trying to form a prayer, any prayer to an invisible God. Once in his youth he had been treed by an angry badger that had gnawed and scraped the trunk for an hour before it gave up and ambled off into the brush. But there were no trees on these mud flats to shimmy up. Cypress stumps and wind-bent willows were next to useless for protection. "Stay on your feet no matter what, and keep your back to mine," he said to Patch, his voice deadly calm with that surge of adrenaline that pours into the human system during emergencies.

And then there was no time for prayer or plead-ing, for a savage golden beast, bigger than any wolf or dog or coyote had a right to be, leaped at Cooper's throat, its gaping jaws and long yellowed fangs grinning. With an inhuman yell, he raised the ax to meet it, slamming the animal's head broadside with the ax, and they could hear the bones in its neck cracking. The impact wrenched the ax from his grip, sending it flying amidst the rest of the pack. But the golden beast came on, propelled by a strength and momentum that exceeded life, its gaping mouth rushing into Cooper's face, the long golden body thudding against his chest, knocking him to his back upon the frozen ground as it collapsed finally atop him.

The pack whirled, jaws snapping as they leaped around the ax. Finding it inanimate, they began to menacingly encircle Patch and Cooper once again. But instinct bred into them during untold generations informed them their leader was dead. Yelping, they scudded on their bellies, moving back into the mists.

Patch did not know the coy-dog was dead, she only saw that it was upon Cooper. She moved swiftly despite the pain in her knee and began to attack the dog as it lay jerking in death throes. She pounded it with her stun stick again and again, and in the confusion Cooper threw his hands up, burrowing deeper beneath the animal to protect himself from Patch's blows. But several slid off the animal. *Good creeping damn!* he thought as Patch thumped him on his shoulder and gasped as the next blow caught his head, sending him into a world of blackness. Patch screamed, fearing he was dying.

The coy-dog was stilled and Patch rolled it away. "Cooper! Cooper! Oh, you can't die on me!" She shook him. "You're my destiny. Open your eyes. Oh, please, open your eyes." She unwound the muffler from his neck, searching for wounds. Finding none, she checked his arms, his hands. No bite marks there, either. Puzzled, sucking in cold air, she leaned back on her heels, at once aware of the throbbing pain in her knee where it had collided with the frozen earth near the muskrat den.

Cooper flicked his eyelids carefully, seeing a kaleidoscope of refracting shapes, one of which was a hazy Patch leaning over him.

"You flat out fainted!" she exclaimed.

"You cracked my skull with that damn stun stick," he returned weakly. "Talk about flailing a dead dog—"

"You killed their leader," Patch gasped, gulping air. "I thought we were dead. You...you saved my life."

"I was saving mine at the same time, or trying to, not that it did me much good." His face pale, he sat up slowly, feeling for the goose-egg-size lump above his brow and touching it tenderly. "Damn! I see two of everything."

Patch located the ax, hobbled painfully back to the canal, chopped out a piece of ice and wrapped it in Cooper's muffler. "Here, put this on your head, it might help. We can't stay out here very long without moving or we'll freeze."

Cooper stood up, getting his bearing, squinting against the pounding in his skull. "My head feels like it wants to float off."

"Don't let it. It's one of the nicest parts about you."

"Jokes from you I don't need." He nudged the carcass of the beast with his boot gingerly. In death its tongue lolled over its wide jaws, obscenely and, Cooper thought, somehow sad.

Then from the reaction—weakness and shock, the sudden draining of energy—his hands began to shake. He shook out the neck wrap and hung it over his shoulders, activity to cover the embarrassing tremors, and turned to Patch.

She had crumpled to the ground and was weeping softly.

He knelt beside her. "Don't go crying on me. We'd better get moving. They might come back and we might not be so lucky next time. Can you walk or shall I carry you?"

"I can walk." She took several steps beside him, then folded to the ground. "My knee..." she cried, grinding her teeth at the pain.

She cradled the ax and the stun stick in her arms while Cooper cradled her in his. The narrow band of light that widened on the horizon in the east shot a pink glow on the melting mists. Cooper increased his pace.

"Look there!" Patch whispered, pointing to a spot some five hundred yards distant.

A mound of vibrant yellow glistened in the new sun. Cooper let Patch slide from his arms. "You stay put until I check it out."

"Take the ax," she cautioned.

"No, whatever it is isn't moving." Or whoever, he thought, dreading what he might find. Patch watched him approach the yellow slash with caution, kneel beside it, then run back to her.

"It's Lafargue and his wife. She's conscious, just barely...said they were heading to our camp when Lafargue keeled over. Both are near frozen." He scooped Patch up into his strong but weary arms, depositing her a moment later next to Una.

Patch put out her hand to the girl. "Una, what's happened?"

"The baby...he is coming," Una gasped.

"Now?" Patch breathed, incredulous, wanting to say how stupid it was for Una to accompany Arlis to camp when she knew her time was so close, biting back the retort because she was obviously frightened, cold and in pain.

"Soon," Una replied, lifting a hand toward Arlis. "Is he...dead?"

Patch looked at Cooper, who was examining Arlis. He shook his head in disgust. "Smells like a brewery. He's passed out."

"Arlis is fine, just sleeping," she related to Una. "But we're in a sorry way." She stretched out her hand to Cooper, speaking softly. "You'll have to take Una to camp first, then come back for me and Arlis."

Cooper protested violently. "I can't leave you. No!" He moved back to Arlis, grabbed the Cajun by his shoulders, shaking him furiously until his head rolled on his neck back and forth, back and forth, to

no avail. Cooper let loose a string of invectives. Una
gave up a discordant moan and that settled it.

"See if you can find some driftwood along that
canal," Patch said, seeing Cooper's look of resignation. She was filled with shame that knowing the
swamp as she did, it had been she who had stumbled
into a hole. "If we had a bit of fire against the chill,
and a few pieces of ice, I can get Arlis awake by the
time you return. It'll take less than an hour, Cooper.
Camp is just around that stand of willows. Follow
the canal."

That the coy-dogs might return was a thought ab-
solutely not to be borne. After the pitifully small fire
was built and Cooper was ready to leave, he knelt
and put his hands upon Patch's shoulders. He drew
her to him, not suddenly or savagely, but gently, his
gaze fixed upon her face. He felt a ragged-edged
stone at the base of his throat, cutting off his breath.
"If.... Damn it. You keep that ax handy...."

"The dogs won't come back," she assured him,
her eyes wide. "It's almost full dawn."

He released her and stood, worried still about her
safety, yet feeling an urge to say something to mark
these moments as unforgettable. Nothing adequate
came to mind. He gathered Una into his arms,
sallied forth several yards, stopping in midstride.
"I've never met a woman like you before," he called
over his shoulder. His voice was that of a man pro-
nouncing an invocation. "I didn't know they ex-
isted...."

"Nor I a man like you," Patch answered, feeling
shivers pass up and down her spine. "Now go!" she
admonished softly, "Or I'll freeze to death while
we're making cow eyes at each other."

She saw him smile, his full lips curving, the
grooves in his face deepening, and could have sworn
that he actually swaggered as he strode off with the

unwieldy Una in his arms. Her gaze stayed with him
until he had disappeared from view. Then, with an
utterly weary sigh, she gave her attention to Arlis
Lafargue.

GOD HAD SCOOPED UP ALL SOUND and put it in *grand-*
mère's trunk—oh! Her own trunk now, yet each
time she opened it to put in a wish a pack of snarling
coy-dogs leaped out at her. She called for help but
Cooper only stood by, his hands folded across his
chest. He was chanting, "Courtesan...courtesan...
courtesan." Then she tried to stop Arlis from climbing into the trunk with the wild dogs, but he spun
like a dervish waving a whiskey bottle. And there
was Rosalina laughing, her wedding veil billowing
in flames while Gaston looked on sorrowfully. Rosalina's laughter closed about Patch's throat like the
silken threads of her pledge, and every laugh caused
a sharp pulsating dart of agony in her knee until she
suddenly emerged into a world filled with sound.

She turned to Cooper to ask him if he heard, but
she couldn't speak. She tried to close her ears, but
the sound was real, febrile, and she opened her eyes,
blinking to shut out the lantern glow. Cooper was
bending over her, calling her name, his face beard
shadowed and weary. It seemed that there was some
task she must do, but all that came to mind was that
she must remember to ask him why his beard came
out so dark when his hair was so fair. She snuggled
deeper into the quilts.

"Patch...you were having a nightmare."

Reality scattered the remnants of the dream. It all
came back, and Patch very quickly mastered the
confusion inside her. "Cooper!" she wailed, mortified. "I must've gone to sleep! How did you manage
to get us back to camp?" She made a clumsy, too-
quick effort to sit up and failed. Cooper plumped her

pillows, slid his arms beneath hers and leaned her against them. His nearness made her heart flutter, and she noted she was undressed down to her long underwear, with the leg of one cut off above her injured knee.

"Carried you over my shoulder and dragged Lafargue by his collar. He's scraped up some. I put him on the sofa, Una's in my bunk." The truth was that he had been filled with panic from the moment he had left her on the mud flats beside that tiny fire. Upon returning he had found her curled up on the frozen mud, an arm thrown out. Dead, he had thought, and he never wanted to go through a moment like that again in his life: yanking open her slicker and the sheepskin jacket beneath it to press his head to her breast. The steady beat of her heart had been a singing in his soul, and he had wanted to lie there with her gathered in his arms forever. But he didn't know how to tell her these things yet. It was enough that she was safe. A miracle that they both were, let alone Arlis and Una.

"Arlis will survive, no doubt," Patch said with a delicate snort of disgust. "And he'll have to live down that an outsider rescued him."

Inspecting Cooper more closely as he sat down beside her, she saw that his face was gaunt, the grooves in his cheeks shadowy thin lines, his eyes sunk far back in their sockets so that they appeared as dark and murky pools. Calm after a storm; calm after the warfare that had raged inside his soul. What was unmistakable was a triumphant glow in those deep-blue depths. "You look so tired. Have you had any rest? And how's your head?" She'd never live *that* down.

"A couple of hundred aspirins ought to take care of my head. I've been trying to keep my eyes open until you woke up. I made Una as comfortable as

I could...drank enough coffee to wet down this whole swamp. You really put a buzz in my head with that stick. If I could just lie back for a minute...."

"Yes, yes," she said haltingly, pulling him down beside her, and in an instant he was beyond the reach of any sound softer than a thunderclap.

The radio was on low. While Cooper lay in her arms Patch listened to the commentator describe the horrors of the worst winter in more than a century. There was a footnote about two hunters frozen to death near Lost Lake. She shook her head in dismay. "You were right," she whispered, thinking the hunter's fates could have been their own. "We shouldn't have gone out this morning." Cooper slept on, but Una began to make noise.

Feeling it indecent that she and Cooper lay in the same bed in another's wakeful presence, Patch rolled out of the bunk, being careful to place her weight on her uninjured leg. Gritting her teeth, she massaged the hurt knee until it was no longer stiff, then made her way to the other woman's side.

Una's skin was parchment pale, her voice weak, her spaniel eyes bleary with resignation. "I'm ahaving this baby, Patch. I warned Arlis it wouldn't be good me coming out here. I warned him...I wanted to stay with ma...." She turned her head and began to sob. "I'm scared...and the pains hurt."

Patch patted Una's arm, an arm that a year ago she would have gladly wrenched from its socket. Now.... She broke the thought. "Try to hold back until the freeze snaps, then most prob'ly we'll get you into Catahoula."

Una emitted a wild noise, half laugh, half gasp as a pain struck. "I can't hold this young'un back. You just better figure on midwifing...." Her breath was coming in gulps between pains and sniffles.

"This is your first," Patch said hesitantly. "It's not going to come all that fast."

"I've been in labor two full days."

"Two?" Patch choked, feeling helpless. "Why didn't you make Arlis take you home before the freeze caught you?"

"He spent one night with the old Indian and his woman, came home drinking and kept on, like he was mad at me or somethin'." She squinted her eyes and grabbed her great belly, panting hard.

When the pain subsided Patch said, "Maybe he's mad at himself."

"Likely he is, seeing as he left you for me and got the short end of the bargain."

Not knowing what to say, Patch made a little business of straightening her head and looking out the window. Lor, but she was thankful she had not exchanged marriage vows with Arlis. Out of the corner of her eye she caught Una watching her, waiting. "Are you hungry, Una?"

"I am a bit, but I been scared to eat. The government man gave me coffee, but he don't make it right."

As she sat beside Una her knee had stiffened up again. Patch worked it gingerly. She glanced at Arlis lying on the sofa, his neck arched backward, mouth gaping open, sleeping like his lights had gone out in a thunderstorm. She shrank from the memory that she'd once thought she loved him, that he had been the first man to touch her, angry that she had not seen his little-man ways. The self-knowledge gave her a sudden sincere compassion for Una. "I'll make some fresh and fix you a bite. You've got to keep your strength, no matter what."

She bathed and dressed hurriedly, keeping a cautious eye on the sofa so that Arlis didn't stir and catch her at it. As she steeped coffee, fried bacon and potatoes, she worried about the baby coming. In spite of all that she knew about nature, Patch was sadly lacking in information about human birthing. She knew how it was supposed to happen, but was unable to imagine the reality.

She gave Cooper a swift critical glance. If it came down to it, he'd have to help.

The sun gave way to the moon, the sky was clear, with millions of stars twinkling in the heavens. A gray shadow flitted past the window. Patch left the stove, going quickly outside to stand a moment on the back deck. She watched the heron until it settled near a drooping willow. Swamp creatures were stirring again! A gust of wind beat around the side of the shanty. She sucked it in. Cold, though not that aching cold that hurt the lungs. She hurried back to the stove, making up a plate for Una.

"Looks like the freeze is breaking," she said as she helped Una struggle to a sitting position. "Might be you'll be having your baby in Catahoula after all, no?"

Una shook her head, her lank brown hair swishing over her shoulders. "I ain't so hungry now. My water's broke. I got your bed all wet and the pains are coming closer, harder, too."

"You're making that up," Patch uttered hoarsely.

"I am not," Una replied with dignity and threw back the quilts. "You feel for yourself."

There was nothing for it then except to help Una out of her clothes, wrap her in a clean blanket while Patch remade the bunk.

"You oughten to put some newspapers under them linens else that mattress ain't going to be fit for nothin' after this baby," Una directed.

Patch ran her fingers distractedly through her curls. "You see anybody delivering papers down this canal?" she snapped, feeling contrite at once for talking so mean. "I'm sorry, Una. Suppose I cut the back out of a slicker?"

"Oughten to work just as well...if'n you hurry it up." There was a kind of stark surprise in the young girl's voice.

Patch looked at the strained expression and suddenly felt hollow inside. "You can't be that close," she said. "You can't...." These last words were uttered fiercely, as if in them alone were gathered all the pleading and prayers spoken in a lifetime.

Her hands flew, cutting out the slicker and easing Una, wearing only one of Cooper's old flannel shirts, down upon the newly made bunk. "You hold back as much as you can," Patch instructed, pulling the quilt up to her neck, "While I get the men up."

"I don't know. I can't keep from pushin' when the pains come, lessen I scream."

"Well, scream then," declared Patch as she went to rouse Arlis.

"Get me some coffee," he ordered, his voice hoarse, his eyes bloodshot with the rheumy look of an old man's.

Patch straightened, her chest swelling. "This is Patch Chauvin you're speaking to, Arlis Lafargue," she announced hotly, not liking him commanding her about as though he owned her. "You can get your own coffee, but not before you wash up. Una is fixing to have your baby, and she needs your help."

In a swift sideways glance she saw Una give Arlis one quick pleading look, then turn away without saying a word.

"Havin' babies is woman's work, no? Ain't anything I kin do." With his tough callused hands he began to rub his arms. "It's a mite chilly in here. Looks like you coulda thought to throw a piece a flannel over me, no?"

Arlis's thoughtlessness, his insensitivity to Una,

his man-tone to herself was too much in the face of all the calamity Patch had been through and that which she was about to face. Seemingly of its own volition, her hand made a tiny fist, drew back then shot forward, connecting with Arlis's long aristocratic nose. His head jerked back, blood spurting as he looked up at her, stunned.

"Lor! What'd you do that for?"

"Arlis Lafargue," she rasped, "you ought not be turned loose in this swamp without a harness! Cooper and I came on you lying out on the mud flats drunk and near frozen with Una in labor. The first words out of your mouth ought to be 'thank you.' If you don't spit them out right this minute, you can take yourself out to the skinning shed and stay there without food or heat until the ice breaks. And after saying thank-you, you can get to the sink, clean up, get yourself coffee, then sit by Una and help her as much as you can."

"You ain't got no call to act like this," Arlis wheedled, his voice sounding strange coming as it did through his bloodied nose.

"You heard the lady," Cooper called soft and low from his bunk. He stretched and gave a long yawn, then bent his eyes once more to Arlis, an expectant look on his face.

Arlis gave one scant restless glance at Patch, looked apprehensively at Cooper, then turned to Una as if for support. But Una was off in her own world of pain. Finally he bowed his shoulders in a shrug. "Thank you for hauling me off the mud flats," he muttered grudgingly.

"I'll say one thing for you, Arlis," Patch sniffed. "When you're between a rock and a hard place, you always take to the rock. Go wash up now, then sit by Una."

When he moved off she watched him with a little head shake.

"Come over here," Cooper called. She went. "How's your knee, and had I better take a look at that hand?" He grinned, and much of the weariness dropped from his face.

"My knee is fine, so's my hand. But Una is in a bad way. Her baby is coming. I don't think Arlis is going to be much help. That leaves you and me."

His face reddened all the way down his corded neck. "I don't know the first thing about bringing babies into the world."

"You know more than I do. You delivered a calf once."

Cooper choked. "It's not the same," he said, catching his breath.

"What you know is more than the rest of us. Besides," she added with a practical lift to her shoulders, "Una will do the hard part."

PATCH WENT OVER IT in her mind for the hundredth time. Kerosene lanterns from the skinning shed had been hung from ceiling beams, spreading light into corners that the bulb over the table didn't reach. On a wooden box draped with a clean cloth lay a knife to cut the cord—boiled to dispense with germs. The portable heater from the drying shed, scrubbed clean and throwing off heat, was close to Una's bunk; one of the bath flannels had been cut in half to wrap the baby. An old flannel shirt, supple and soft as silk, had been ripped apart—ready for cleaning the baby and Una. And sanitary pads from her personals kit. Those she had secreted under her sweater as she'd moved across the room and hidden them under a blanket, talking to distract the men from what she was doing. Her mind registered that the napkins were necessary, yet allowing Cooper and Arlis to see them seemed somehow too intimate.

Mouth agape, Una moaned and screamed as if she could expel the grinding ache in her loins along with each gush of air. With every pain Patch gritted her teeth in sympathy, and as the pain died, Patch cooed gently to Una, wiping away perspiration that beaded on her forehead.

"What time is it?" asked Una weakly.

Patch twisted about, looking at the clock. "Eleven-twenty. Your pains are coming about two minutes apart now."

"That ain't why I wanted to know," Una panted. "If'n I can hold back just a little, my baby'll be born on Christmas." Her wide mouth curved against another great pull in her belly. "That'll be a Christmas present Arlis...won't...be able to match... no?" She gritted her teeth at the pain, face distorted, lost now to everything outside the pulsating new life trying to free itself from her womb.

Christmas! Patch felt a wailing in her heart. The past days had sped by; she had not been conscious of them, marked as they had been by her misery and Cooper's reserve toward her.

She signaled Arlis to relieve her and left Una's side to pour herself a coffee, then sat on the foot of her bunk, eyes unfocused as one hand traced the ancient brass trim on the old trunk. Her gaze met Cooper's once and slid away, but there was something strange, a sign he couldn't read in her eyes. He crossed the room and sat down beside her on the bunk.

"Is something going wrong over there?" he asked, nodding imperceptibly toward where Arlis now talked quietly to Una. A threat of alarm was building deep in his gut.

Patch shook her head slowly in dismay, making

her thick, richly brown curls catch golden glints
from the wavering flames in the kerosene lanterns.
"Tomorrow..." she swallowed. "Tonight is Christmas Eve. I don't think Gaston made it out of the
swamp to see Rosalina. He couldn't have!" she added fiercely, a catch in her throat. "I so wanted him to
convince her to come home, to marry...." She
shrank from the idea that Rosalina might have refused yet again.

"Don't go buying disappointment," Cooper suggested. "Lord knows I've done it often enough
myself—anticipating the worst. Gaston seems a determined young man. Maybe he got out before the
freeze." He wanted to tell her then and there that he
would wait for her to honor her pledge to her sister,
but the words just hung in his throat. He watched
her fingers unconsciously trail over the old portmanteau as though she were stroking an old friend.
He was thinking of her fingers touching him, caressing his flesh, seeing himself mounted between her
thighs, her body suppliant, moving in rhythm with
his, her voice throaty with passion—wanting him,
needing him, as much as he needed her. "What's in
that old trunk?" he asked, to distract his mind from
the primitive direction it was taking.

She jerked her head as if slapped, her fingers going still. "The dreams and wishes of several life-
times," she said quietly.

Cooper could think of nothing to say. They sat together, minute after minute, without further speech,
each deep in thought. "Look at Arlis," Patch said at
last without the least emotion. "Down on his knees at
Una's side. He never even kneels in church, but always stands at the back as if God had a switch ready."

"He's just nervous," reflected Cooper. "He hasn't
sat still five minutes since he woke up. It's natural, I
suppose, for an expectant father."

"Patch!" Arlis called, sounding strangled. "I think it's time. You better git over here, no?"

"I'm coming, Arlis." She held out her hands, palms up, inspecting them, then turned to Cooper. "You'll have to catch the baby. Mine are too callused, too hard for handling new skin."

He took one, tracing the calluses gently with his forefinger. "You have beautiful hands, dainty, tough—" He turned it over, running a finger over her knuckles. "Scraped up a bit from fighting," he teased. "After seeing you thump Arlis, I'm thinking I'd better watch myself. You're feisty."

"You're making fun of me, *m'sieu.*"

"I'm begging you in the only way I know, not to put me on the business end of Una."

Patch went for the baby lotion, spending a few numbing minutes rubbing it into her hands.

UNA HAD STOPPED SCREAMING, all of her energy being directed to expelling the baby. "I can't hold back!" she moaned, kicking off the quilts and grabbing the back of her knees for leverage as she strained.

"Suffering saints save us!" muttered Arlis. He started to cry, burying his head in the pillows as a tiny dark head began to show itself.

Kneeling between Una's legs, Patch watched in awe as the tiny head receded and came forth again. She glanced once at Cooper, and when he nodded, she slid her hand beneath the baby's head, supporting it. He smiled his approval. "You're doing great," he crooned, as much for Una's benefit as for Patch's.

"I never want to have a baby and go through what Una's suffering," she whispered. Arlis's shoulders were heaving with fearful sobs. He was making more racket than Una. "Coax him to the sofa," Patch begged. "He's distracting Una."

Cooper half dragged, half carried the shaken

Cajun, but he refused to sit. Though it went against the grain, Cooper finally offered him whiskey from his duffel, which quieted Arlis at once.

"Push hard, Una," Patch pleaded, scared now that the baby was only exposed down to its shoulders and seemed to be stuck there.

"I'm...so...tired..," whimpered Una, the jerking muscles in her legs giving truth to her words.

"Just one more push and it'll all be over. Please, Una." Sweat ran in rivulets down Patch's face and neck, her hands trembled holding the tiny neck and head, and her knees felt on fire from being pressed into the hard mattress for so long, especially the one that she had hurt. She turned frightened eyes to Cooper. "Talk to her," she insisted. "She's stopping, and the baby is only halfway here."

Cooper knelt where Arlis had and began to talk softly to Una, asking her what name she had chosen for the baby, did she want a boy or a girl, and if only she would give one more great push she'd know which she had. Patch was almost jealous of the soothing balm of words he pressed on Una.

"I can't do any more," Una croaked, even as another contraction seized her. Nature took over and the baby slipped quickly into Patch's waiting hands.

Excited, stunned, Patch yelled, "I've got it. I've got it! Una, look! It's...it's a girl."

"Looks like a six-pounder. Lay it across Una's stomach," Cooper said, grinning at Patch. "We'd better get the cord cut and tied, and clean out the baby's mouth. Where's that swab we rigged up?"

"You got no call to name my baby an it," noted Una testily.

Cooper apologized. Together he and Patch worked swiftly, doing what had to be done while Arlis kept calling, "Is it over?" Una opened her eyes, smiled at her new daughter, then gave her body over to another contraction.

"Oh, lor!" Patch nearly fainted. "She's having another—"

"That's the afterbirth," said Cooper swiftly, seeing Patch go pale. "Wrap it in the slicker you cut up and I'll dispose of it." He laid the flannel-wrapped baby in the crook of Una's arm. "Think you can look after your daughter a minute while Patch cleans you up?"

Arlis crept back and bent over Una, peeking at the baby. "I wanted a boy."

Patch opened her mouth to rail at his unmitigated gall, but Una got there first and said it profoundly. "I got me a daughter, Arlis, whether you like it or not. I'm sick to death of your soulless complainin'. We ain't even married yet, no? As soon's I'm able, I'm gettin' up from this birthing and going home to my *maman*. All you do anyways is quibble and drink."

"Wait a minute." There was a cautious, placatory note to his voice, a first, Patch was certain as she listened to the exchange. "I was wantin' a boy, but I didn't say a girl wouldn't do."

"As good as said it," Una retorted, a lioness with a protective paw about her cub. Patch was thinking that Una had made her last apology.

Arlis stumbled over his next words. "We'll get married before we get her baptised, yes?"

"It's somethin' to think about," Una replied with a degree less truculence and turned her attention to the curly dark-haired bundle in her arms as the baby tried out her vocal cords for the first time.

Her eyes still bright with wonder that she had shared the moment of its birth, Patch watched the tiny mouth quiver, heard the tiny voice, hardly more than a sparrow squawk. Very carefully she touched the baby's hand with a fingertip.

"Your time'll be around the corner," Una said tranquilly.

Patch pulled the quilts up to Una's neck and sighed deeply. "Think you'll be okay for a while?" she asked, feeling exhaustion creep over her like a hundred-legged centipede. "I have to lie down for a few minutes."

"I'm fine now, I had my baby on Christmas," Una assured her, then shyly said, "I'm not the leastways mad at you for thunkin' Arlis, he had it comin'." She smiled shyly. "Might be I'll take up the habit myself, seeing as how much good it done."

"I didn't mean to, it just happened."

"Felt like you meant it," Arlis put in. Patch ignored him. He was Una's problem now.

"Anyways, thank you," said the new mother.

"You're welcome," Patch returned, and she was on her bunk before she realized she didn't know if the thank you was for being a midwife or for coming out long in the set-to with Arlis.

With an arm crooked over her eyes she reviewed her day, her life, sorting it into various pieces— beginnings, endings and between. Cooper was the between. Her heart swelled with wanting of him, hungry for his strength, his tenderness, too, now that she had glimpsed it in his caring for Una. To have a man like that beside her for the rest of her days.... A lump grew in her throat, lodging there until she turned into her pillow and swallowed it back. It was all up to God now, and no doubt, after performing one miracle in the tar-papered shack tonight, He had no time for another.

"You going off to sleep?" Cooper's voice came from a low deep place, threaded with emotion. Patch turned over, her hip meeting his as he lowered himself next to her.

"Not if you want to talk. I felt exhaustion there for a few minutes."

"Still think you don't want to have any babies?"

"I—not if I have to deliver it myself." She swallowed to control the husky tremor in her voice, waiting for him to say more, waiting for him to say he wanted her to bear his children.

Cooper was wondering if she was aware of the irresistible power she held over him, and he wished that they were alone so that he could rid himself of this burning in his loins. "We've had a busy twenty-four hours, haven't we?"

"You're as tired as I am, no? You want to stretch out next to me? Under the circumstances...."

A muscle tightened in his jaw. "I don't think that would be wise. Lying next to you would be more than I could handle just now. I'll claim the sofa for a couple of hours while Arlis acquaints himself with his new daughter."

Patch clutched the quilt a little more tightly to her, wishing it were the only barrier between them. "First one up wakes the other?"

"Good enough." He hesitated and rubbed his forehead. "I don't suppose a quick kiss would be out of order?"

She glanced at the threesome in the opposite corner. The adults' attention was all for their baby. "I don't suppose," she replied throatily, and parted her lips in welcome, seeking the thrust of his tongue as his mouth descended.

Moments later when she drifted off to sleep, she flirted with a fragile flame of hope. There was always the old trunk, and Grand-mère Duval, for all her foolish sayings, hadn't seemed disappointed with the wishes and longing she had deposited there.

13

PATCH DID NOT FLOURISH in chaos and spent the morning putting the shack into manageable disorder. What with herself, Cooper, Arlis, Una and the baby, the place was filled to overflowing—though at this minute the intruders were crowded together on the far bunk, where Una was trying to get her daughter to take her nipple. Patch kept her eyes away from that, hoping Cooper would, too. All the attention was going to the baby, and though she didn't begrudge it, she was feeling left out.

"That melancholy expression on your face says you don't exactly have the Christmas spirit," Cooper said quietly as he finished shaving and patted after-shave on his cheeks. "Is there anything I can do to help?"

The woodsy fragrance made breathtaking yearnings skim along the surface of Patch's flesh. Her expression took on a faraway look, dark eyes shadowed by the harsh lighting from the bare overhanging bulb. She answered testily, "Not unless you can conjure me up some privacy."

Cooper edged closer and put his arm about her waist, drawing her intimately close. "For the two of us, or just yourself?"

At his touch her heart began to beat with an odd rhythm; hard, soft, starting up again. Cloves that she was pressing into a smoked ham spilled from her fingers, scattering haphazardly upon the honey-rubbed pork. She tried to lighten the feeling that was knotting her nerves.

"I wish Indian Jack had made it. I have the crab-meat stuffing all made and no flounder."

"That's what I call changing the subject. Are you wishing now that I'd never come?"

She stood silently for a moment, then took a deep breath that did nothing to calm the mallet pounding on her heart. "I could never wish such a thing, but it's not like you were staying permanent...."

"You know I'm not good with words, yet I don't think I can live without you. Does that tell you anything?"

"It tells me my whole being is filling up with want of you," she whispered.

"Yes, well," he muttered wryly, putting a little distance between them. "There's a part of me filling up, too."

Patch sank into the nearest chair. "If only Gaston got out before the freeze," she said wistfully. "He could be talking to Rosalina this exact minute."

Cooper leaned against the sink counter, glancing out the window, noting the bright sun, melting ice, a lone pelican skimming low over a canal, before he turned back to Patch. "I'm an impatient man, but if Gaston didn't make it—or even if he did and your sister is still being stubborn, though I imagine that's a family trait—we'll go to Baton Rouge ourselves. She has to look presentable by now. How many operations has she had?"

"So many...so many I've lost count. *Maman* knows, but if we mention going...." Troubled, she concentrated on picking up the scattered spice.

A gaze of steely determination flickered in Cooper's blue eyes. "We'll go and we'll convince her to come home. I won't ask you to break your word of honor, but...." He flung a hand in the direction of the couple on the far side of the shack. By now he knew that Patch had been jilted by Arlis for Una, knew that those two weren't wed, but these facts paled in comparison to what he felt for Patch. He took a deep breath. There was about Patch a quality of grim endurance that he felt more and more he could not match. "I'd like a family, too." A blush worked up his thickly corded neck as if he'd been caught in an unforgivable social blunder.

"Wha—" Patch bolted up. "What are you saying, *m'sieu?*"

He laughed gently. "Old habits die hard, don't they? But I don't want an audience for this conversation. Let's save it for later."

"You're making riddles," she snipped, her voice trembling a little, rife with disappointment that he had brushed off the topic when she was so eager for the promise it held, hanging on every word. Still, the melancholy was gone from her expression. The sudden gushing of water from the sink tap made her start.

"Oh! The ice in the rain barrel has melted. I must've left the spigot open." It was a sign. She just knew it. All at once Christmas dinner seemed very important. She began to bustle between the stove and the table, doing busy work in a kind of frenzied gaiety to camouflage her hope.

A pristine white tablecloth brought from her mother's house was spread upon the old scarred table. Red bayberry candles, stuck on saucers, were lit, sending a festive aroma into the air. And while the ham browned, sweet potatoes baked and blackberry dumplings boiled down, Cooper brought out his bottle of whiskey. Even Una took a small sip though she feared making the baby drunk on her milk.

Patch heard the motor before the rest of them. She put down her glass and flew to the door, swinging it open. "It's Indian Jack, coming down the bayou in

194   *Beneath a Saffron Sky*

his big steel-bottomed boat, cutting through ice like
it was only spume!"

She grabbed up her jacket and went out to the
wharf to greet him.

"Them dumplings ready?" He handed her a bucket
filled with fish, cleaned and filleted.

"They will be," Patch said, nodding to Indian
Jack's woman. "I'm running a little late on dinner.
Had to deliver Una's baby first."

"Is that a fact?" Indian Jack replied just as casually. "Arlis is here, too?"

"Found them both freezing out on the bog at
dawn yesterday."

"Baby?" exclaimed Indian Jack's woman, hurrying past them into the shack.

"Strangest things loosen a woman's tongue," said
the old Indian.

There were greetings all around. Indian Jack inspected the baby, which now resided in his wife's
arms while Una looked on anxiously. Feet, hands,
navel were given a close scrutiny. "Clara says fine
job!"

"Clara? That's your name?" Patch inquired.

"Since I was born myself."

Indian Jack moaned momentously. "Never get her
to keep shut now." He turned to Arlis. "How's your
backside? You sittin' yet?"

Patch whirled from the sink where she was washing the fish. "Arlis hasn't been sitting. Standing,
kneeling and lying down, but not sitting. What's
wrong with you, Arlis?" Her eyes were enflamed,
but she suddenly knew the answer. Deep down inside she knew it.

"Arlis took a load of buckshot, an accident," said
Indian Jack.

Everyone stopped and looked at Arlis. A knife
materialized in Patch's hand. Cooper stepped up to

her. Good creeping damn! "Own up, Lafargue, and let's get this done with," he said. "I'm hungry."

Arlis eyed the knife. "I was only taking what was rightfully mine. Patch and I are betrothed, the banns were read. She promised we'd trap together."

A rising surge of anger flushed Patch's cheeks. "Making a baby with Una undid your promises to me and mine to you! You're lower than a snake, Arlis. I ought to—"

Cooper grabbed her hand, twisting the knife from it. "Now look, if there's anything I can't abide, it's tantrums on Christmas."

"This is no trantrum!"

"It's revenge, Patch. Arlis is Una's problem now. Let it be. I imagine once word gets around, Arlis'll have his hands full explaining to other trappers how he got a load of buckshot in his backside. That'll clip his feathers some. What do you say, Indian Jack?"

His beady eyes bore down on Arlis. "Don't think it'd be too healthy for you to go wandering around in the swamp after dark. A person might think you was a poacher and let loose with more than buckshot."

"You can't prove nothin'," whined Arlis.

"Who needs to prove up a dead poacher?" canted Indian Jack with finality, and Arlis slunk off to Una's corner. She moved off the bunk and sat with Clara on the sofa.

At first dinner was subdued, but Indian Jack began with his stories, Patch recalled other Christmases in the shack and along the bayou, and soon they were singing carols along with the radio. Una filled a plate of food for Arlis, which he ate sitting on the sofa. Otherwise no one paid him any mind. After dishes were done with Clara's help, Patch put on her jacket and went outside. Cooper fell in step with her. The sun was disappearing over the western horizon, trailing fingers of purple and gold over the cypress stumps as though giving them benediction before the dark of night closed in. The myriad of rustlings that made up swamp music played like a melody on Patch's ears. The fearsome silence of the freeze was like a bad dream, remembered vaguely, but not painfully. "Seems impossible that it was only yesterday we were out on frozen bog," she said, eyeing the black water that was beginning to move swiftly in the middle of the bayou.

"I know the feeling," admitted Cooper, inhaling deeply.

Expelling a soft sigh, Patch thought she was experiencing one of those moments in life when a person thinks about everything and yet really thinks of nothing. Nothing that is remembered anyway. Little things, perhaps.

Cooper lit a cigarette, propped against a wharf piling to smoke and watched the deepening shadows sculpt Patch's face. "You're really beautiful," he said.

She dropped him an elusive smile. "No one but you has ever said that to me."

"I mean on the inside, too. Vows, delivering babies, trapping, shooting poachers, supporting your family—that makes a man stop and think."

A shiver ran down her spine. He must mean she was expecting any man she took up with to take on her responsibilities. "Scares him, you mean, prob'ly."

A long pondering moment passed before he answered. "Makes a man wonder if he measures up."

For an instant Patch was speechless, finding her tongue only when it registered what he was seeking. "You measure up," she said shyly, her voice thick and melodious. "You fought off the coy-dogs, saving me from certain death. You saved Arlis and Una from freezing. You saved Arlis twice!" she said, recalling the scene and her anger before dinner. "You're perfect."

"I'm far from perfect. You make life bearable for me. I understand things better. I even understand you a little."

"You haven't made up your mind about me, have you? You say you can't live without me, but you're holding back."

"That's not fair. You pull me to you with one hand and push me away with the other. That confuses me. I don't have roots. I can put them down anywhere and let them grow." His voice tightened suddenly. "Say you'll marry me—"

She waved a hand, deflecting his words, her dark eyes huge and liquid ebony, seeming to take up her face. "It's cruel of you to ask me now," she moaned, turning away.

He caught her before she could take a step, his fingers clutching her shoulders so tightly she felt them through the thickness of her jacket. "Patch... let's not end today this way. Let's not spoil it. I've been through a lifetime of miserable lonely Christmases. This was the nicest one I've ever had—if you leave out Arlis—and I can. No tinsel, no trees, no artificiality, no presents, yet the gift of sharing laughter at the table, the singing of carols, holding a baby I helped bring into the world. Waking up this morning to the smell of fried apples and bacon... our first Christmas together—" He broke off, his lids shuttering his eyes for only a second before they pierced her again. "I want to marry you, but more than that right this minute, I want very much to kiss you."

It was a long speech for him, and it had come from his heart. Aching for the pain he had suffered, though some of the ache was for herself, Patch relented, raising her face to his, her arms to his chest, letting her fingers curl about his neck. "I want to kiss you, too, I want—"

He pressed his lips to hers hungrily, almost brutally, his hands leaving her shoulders to slip beneath her coat and knead her waist, the flesh on her back as if she were malleable clay to be formed and made a part of himself.

Patch's body, her mind, were one with Cooper's, making a strange wild sensation course through her, a sensation that took on a shape, a life of its own. Walls that had enclosed Cooper engulfed her, too, like a soft wool cloak of the best quality, rich and warm, protective. She squeezed her eyes to keep back quick salty tears.

It was a kiss that went on and on, and when Cooper finally dragged his mouth from hers, he gave a low moan that articulated all that he felt. He reached for her hand, his eyes somber. "Put a wish in your little trunk for me," he said balefully. "That it's tomorrow and we're alone."

"Is that a Christmas wish?"

"It's a forever wish," he said, and smiled into her great dark eyes.

"Ya'll finished so a man can come outside and get into his boat and go to his camp to sleep off a meal?"

Patch moved quickly away from Cooper's arms. "You're not leaving so soon, Jack?"

"Have to. Got to get the old woman back to camp before she turns into a motor mouth, wantin' this and that."

Clara followed him out. "Bring me back some knitting yarn from Catahoula when you go in, Patch. I'll knit up something for the baby."

"See?" Indian Jack exclaimed glumly.

Patch laughed and waved as they moved off down the bayou.

IT WAS DAWN. Sparrows that sheltered under the eaves of the skinning shed were unbelievably noisy—cheering the vagrant sliver of sun that crept up the old gray walls. Trying to be quiet about it, Patch dressed, drew water for coffee, lit the stove and set it to boiling. Arlis and Una lay together on the far bunk, Cooper was on the sofa, and the baby was sleeping in a box Cooper had hammered together, lining it with furs and quilts. She didn't want to wake the others yet, cherishing the moment of early-morning privacy to get her chores and her thought for the day in order. If the chaos in her hurt mind could be called thinking.

She had lain awake most of the night hoping that Gaston would show up. As the night wore into dawn her hope had died, being replaced by a sharp thrust of despair that clung to her even now. She did not regret her promise to Rosalina. She couldn't; it had been the lodestar upon which she had fixed her goal, and she meant to keep her word. She took a long sip of coffee, staring into the cup as was her habit when thinking. How could she induce Cooper to wait? She was unsure now if it was even fair to ask him.

She took a quick breath and in her mind's eye she could see Rosalina married to Gaston, herself to Cooper. She could see her head bent to Rosalina's ear with the sharing of secrets about their men, their children, as only sisters can. A small smile played about her lips as she hugged her arms around herself, swelling inside with a happy feeling that the daydream nurtured.

It was full light before she knew it, with Cooper up and breakfast smells setting Arlis and Una to stirring. She tried not to hear the low-voiced cooing coming from their corner and spoke hurriedly to Cooper when he returned from starting the generator. With the baby there, doors had to be kept closed, and they needed the light.

"While you take Arlis in the big boat to get his rig, I'll retrieve the pirogue before a high tide comes and floats it off. Una wants to take the baby to her mother's. We'll have to follow them in to Catahoula to sign depositions about the birthing for parish records."

Cooper pulled a chair from the table and sat down purposely. "Do we have to follow them in today? Wouldn't tomorrow do just as well? Or even after the holidays are over as you originally planned?"

"The quicker we get that done the less truck I'll have to have with Arlis, and that suits me fierce," she answered with feeling. Soft giggles came from Una, making them both glance toward that bunk, then look away quickly. Patch's face flamed.

"They ought not be carrying on like that so soon after—"

"I imagine it's all rather innocent." Cooper's tone was dry. "About what I was saying...." His voice was very deliberate—purposefully deliberate—when he continued. "Can't we wait a day or two before going into Catahoula?"

She caught the hooded look beneath his thick fringe of blond lashes. Her back stiffened, her demeanor growing aloof. "All you have on your mind is what those two do," she said loftily.

"I won't deny that's at the back of my mind, but I

thought we'd make some plans. It'd be impossible at your mother's—"

"There's no use making plans until I know about Rosalina. Besides, I want to sell my furs, and I have to talk to *maman* about—"

A sudden roar like a powerful wind careening up from the Gulf filled the shack. The baby began to squeal. Cooper jumped up. "What the hell...?"

"An airboat." Patch tilted her head, a listening posture. "It's Parker's. I can tell. One blade is snapped off and the whirring is uneven. Must be somebody in trouble, else he wouldn't be pushing it that hard." She grabbed up her coat and went flying out the front door.

But it wasn't Parker Voisin sitting in the metal chair in front of the great whirring blades. It was Gaston, and he was coming *up* the bayou from Catahoula.

Patch's chest tightened, and she felt a singing in her heart. She sprang from the wharf onto her boat, leaning over the water to catch the mooring rope as Gaston shut down the machine. In the sudden quiet, the very air seemed to hold its breath.

As she bent low to secure the airboat, Patch's eye caught the gaily wrapped package she had sent with Gaston lying at his feet. He had failed! She felt an unbearable pain pressing her chest. She straightened, opening her mouth to offer consolation, and stopped.

A terrible sadness was in Gaston's eyes, a pathetic yearning in his expression. His young face looked old, his shoulders as bent and rounded as Grandmère Duval's. Beneath his open jacket he was wearing his gray funeral and wedding suit and a white shirt, its pointed starched collar lifted straight out like the crumpled wings of a dove. He dropped his hands from the throttle stick, letting them just hang at his sides, and he made no move to get off the seat. "I was too late." He gazed at Patch and his lashes flickered, picking up Cooper behind her on the wharf. Then his eyes appeared to glaze with shadows.

Patch swallowed over a hard lump that lodged in her throat. "What happened?"

"Happened?" Gaston repeated, sounding lost.

Patch turned to Cooper. "Help me get him into the shack. It's...it's as though he got this far and can't make himself go another inch."

Like a somnambulist, Gaston was easily led. Together they carried him in and put him on the sofa. Arlis was still abed, but Una was at the table, the baby crooked in her arm. Patch signaled silently for her to bring Gaston a coffee. When it was brought she put it in his hands. "Drink, Gaston," she ordered in Cajun French. "It'll warm you."

Her use of the old language seemed to jolt him, and a look of unbelief sprang into his dark eyes. "Rosalina is dead," he stated.

Patch glanced at Cooper, whose eyes seemed to touch her with sympathy. Una made a tight little sound. Patch's gaze flew back to Gaston, and she stared at him with bereft horror. "You mean her love for you—" she began, her voice growing hoarse.

"I mean, she's dead! Dead! More than a year ago!" he screamed, tears beginning to stream down his young-old face.

"You know not what you say, Gaston. Rosalina is... *maman* would have told me—us." Her entire world was shattering around her. She grasped him by his shoulders, shaking him. "You lie, Gaston. You lie! She wrote letters! *Maman* talked with her! *Maman* saw her every month!"

Sobs caught in Gaston's throat, and he held up a hand to deflect her protestations until he could find a stable voice. "She wasn't at the hospital, had not been since December 8 of last year. I argued with them to no avail. I went to the rest home you mentioned to me, but she had never been there—never! I went back to the hospital...waited hours in Administration for someone who could check records. Rosalina...they had the name of the funeral house that had picked up her...her body...I called and found the name of the cemetery...there was a sexton on duty...he showed me her grave. Your *maman*—" he swallowed then, hard "—your *maman* goes there every month to clean the grave, lay fresh flowers. She had been there Christmas Day before I arrived...." His voice faltered; an inhuman sound of grief escaped his throat. "My Rosalina...my gentle heart, my gentle heart," he sobbed, crying unashamedly as only a strong man can.

Patch felt hollow; her brain was denying the truth. She swayed on her feet, appealing to Cooper with a burning gaze. "It isn't true. Rosalina is alive, having another operation in a different hospital, that's all."

Gaston lifted his tear-streaked face, rage displacing his tears. "Your *maman*! Ask her! She wouldn't see me. Grand-mère Duval sent me away."

"I think he's speaking the truth," Cooper said. His voice was quiet and strong.

"No. No he isn't," she whispered. "Rosalina just refused to see him, and so he's made it all up. He was always the one among us who played pranks."

Gaston spoke, parroting words like a dying mimic. "'Rosalina Evangaline Chauvin, gay and spirited daughter of Natalie and Pierre, born June 11, 1951. Died December 8'...carved on the gravestone," he said, choking with sobs. "An angel with fluttering wings of marble." His voice was barely real.

Patch was paralyzed a moment, unable to shift her

feet, and then by some sudden alchemy her legs melted. She managed to take a step back, no more. A heavy weight pressed down upon her, so that her body refused to function at her will. A great gaping ache was filling her, displacing her insides. She grabbed at her stomach, as if to prevent it from spilling out of her flesh. "She can't be dead. My vow . . . she's to come home. . . ."

Gaston reached out a hand as she crumpled, but Cooper was swifter, scooping her up and depositing her on her bunk. But Patch had not fainted, only crossed into a world of different dimensions.

Her voice seemed to break as if it were crystalline, her lips moving, quivering with remembrances, softly lilting snatches of anecdotes, pieces of life she had shared with her sister. But no tears came as she rocked back and forth, a metronome in agony.

While she rocked, oblivious to him, Cooper did what he could to make her comfortable. Protectiveness overwhelmed him, coupled with a sense of helplessness that no one could suffer grief for another. He hurt for her. He knew how much she had loved Rosalina, recalling instantly the night she had spoken of Rosalina in the skinning shed, her voice soft, eyes glowing. And now her eyes were dulled, opaque. He removed her jacket, the moccasins she wore inside the shack, tenderly touching her cap of dark curls, her eyelids, squeezing her shoulder to let her know he was there. He felt a stirring between his legs, cursing himself that he should want her so at a time like this, chafing that there were others about. If only he could love her, absorb some of her pain. He wanted to ravage her until she screamed, until she poured it all out. He tried to read her eyes, but they were like shimmering onyx, lit only from inward visions. . . .

Propriety be damned, he thought, as he took her into his arms, rocking with her, and every inch of her seemed to taunt him. He happened to glance up and caught Una's pensive stare. The new mother glided quietly to him, the baby cradled in her arm.

"If there is any whiskey left, perhaps a small sip for Gaston, *m'sieu*? And then Arlis will load the boat with the furs. We can travel all together on Patch's boat. Later Arlis can get his papa to bring him back."

Cooper nodded even as his arms tightened around Patch. "That will be fine. Thank you."

"It is no more than you have done for me—for us." She smiled down at her daughter, then looked back at Patch, her expression sorrowful. "Rosalina was friend to me...*amie*...we were in school together. One can't help but wonder what it was that made Madam Chauvin keep such a dreadful secret...."

Yes, Cooper thought, one can't help but wonder. He was reminded of his own mother, and the subtle poison her abandonment had caused to course through his veins. He had never believed that things happened fairly in life. He had seen too much, suffered too much injustice in his own life for that. But he had had a new sense of freedom—from hate and bitterness—since he had been able to talk of his past. He wanted that now for Patch. He pressed his lips to her hair, listening to her whimper, and couldn't help wondering what this sad turn of events meant for him, for her, for them both.

"You must take her to the old woman, Grand-mère Duval, no?" said Una, misinterpreting his silence. "She will know what to do."

He knew Patch had been terribly offended that Arlis had jilted her for Una. As he looked at the woman now he saw decency and integrity there, far more than Arlis Lafargue deserved. "I'll take her," he said, and his voice trembled, electrified at the sudden possibilities.

Bales of furs were used to build a windbreak on the prow of the boat to protect Patch, Una and the baby from the cutting wind, which was always greater on the water. Patch was shamed by the weakness that made it necessary for Cooper to help her into the boat. She could not shake the fugue that had descended upon her; her body felt worn, limbs leaden, nerves torn, energy nonexistent. She wanted to explain this to Cooper as he tucked blankets about her but she had no words. She just sat and looked at him, too exhausted with grief to think or speak.

"You're in shock. It's to be expected," he told her as if reading her mind. "Now just lean back, rest if you can."

She wanted to reach out and grasp Cooper with her heart, but she couldn't do that, either. In the end she drooped against the scratchy hemp sacks and closed her eyes, listening to the starting-up activity that went on about her.

Cooper reluctantly shifted his gaze from Patch to clasp Gaston on the shoulder, smiling to quell the anxiety he himself felt. "Thanks for helping us load up. Sure you won't change your mind and come with us back to town?"

Gaston shook his head. "There'll be pandemonium at my brother's house what with it being the day after Christmas...and too many people. This is a sad burden for me, I don't want to share it. Everyone will say, 'You're young, you'll get over it. Time is a great healer.'" His lips twisted in a sad smile. "That's what they said when my *maman* died. I still miss her, too. The camp is better, and quiet." His eyes were welling up with tears again.

Cooper looked away, embarrassed, wishing he

could express his own sorrow that way, for if he could he would cry for Patch.

Gaston sniffed and took a deep breath. "I share this with you. Rosalina and I were married in the eyes of God—twice," he said liltingly, and a little flush came into his sunken gray cheeks as he revealed this. "You must tell Patch when she is able to listen. It might help her." His voice grew almost inaudible. "The memory of it is helping me."

Cooper swallowed back a lump that was forming in his throat. "Of course, I'll tell her."

Arlis started the motor of the working launch, anxious now to return to Catahoula. He had a daughter to show off. Gaston glanced once at Patch, then urged Cooper onto the boat as if now he was in a hurry to get on with the loneliness that weighed heavily upon his soul. "I'll batten down your camp before I leave."

"Take whatever you need," Cooper admonished, thanking him. Familiar with the swamp now, he stepped off the wharf and took the tiller from Gaston. During the trip down the bayou there was no sound except the noise of the motor and the slapping of the waves, and for a while, the baby crying.

15

PATCH RALLIED FROM HER LETHARGY to kiss the baby when Arlis and Una disembarked at the leaning ragged wharf in front of Una's mother's house. As Cooper guided the boat back to midstream she went to sit next to him at the stern. Her heart hammered, her pulse throbbed, her throat ached. She dreaded the confrontation with *maman*, envying Una at that moment who was bringing a gift, a granddaughter to her mother, while she herself had only a question to offer Natalie—why?

Eyeing her anxiously, Cooper turned down the motor so that they could talk. "I hate seeing you so unhappy like this. You could be right, you know. Rosalina might have been moved to another hospital."

She widened her eyes to keep tears from spilling over. "Cooper...."

"Never mind, it was a dumb thing to say."

"No, it wasn't. I wanted to believe that, too, but hope is a refuge only for those who won't face facts. I just wish...." She glanced away, a distant look in her eyes, sighing. "Wishing is a refuge, too."

He was happy to have her talking, making sense, and he shuddered slightly at the memory of her rocking on her bunk in camp. He'd thought she might never be whole again.

"Are you cold?"

He smiled warmly at her. "No, not a bit." And as they drew near the wharf at her mother's house he noticed that her skin was pale, the look on her face one of total desolation, but her eyes were alive. He couldn't ask for more than that, considering....

The wind gusted in the dogtrot, setting the pine-cone-and-ribbon wreaths on each door to rattling. Touching tenderly with a gloved hand the red plaid streamers and tiny papier-mâché birds, Patch murmured, "Rosalina made these." She bent her head, stifling a sob. "Oh, Cooper, there's so little of her left. Nothing will ever be the same again."

Her stricken face made Cooper wince with anger at the injustice in the world. He cleared his throat in an effort to sound resolute. "She lives in you, in your memory of her." It was all he could think to say.

Because Patch trembled with a chill that had little to do with the wind, he put his hand tenderly under her elbow and ushered them into the parlor.

A fire burned low in the grate. Grand-mère Duval dozed in her rocking chair, but *maman* was nowhere about. Patch touched the old woman's shoulder, shaking her gently, and she looked up with faded eyes mirroring the dreadful melancholy in Patch's expression.

"Gaston was here," she stated in her cracked old voice. "You know of Rosalina, no?"

"You knew all the time, didn't you, *grand-mère*?"

"I guessed. I saw her troubled spirit soaring with Duval's."

"I want to see *maman*. Where is she?"

"In her room. She hasn't come out since Gaston—"

The parlor door swung open. "I heard the boat," said Natalie, looking past Cooper to her daughter.

Patch was shocked at her mother's appearance. Her hair, usually so tidy, was flyaway, her sweater was buttoned wrong. Her face looked ravaged, drawn with wrinkles Patch had never noticed before, and she was leaning on the cane papa had carved but pride had kept her from using in front of others.

Cooper stood near the fire warming his hands, trying to understand what the rules were in a situation like this, fathoming the boundaries he must stay within. After a first glance at Natalie he had eyes only for Patch, and he sensed a pain deep in her soul. He gleaned then that this was a thing she must, *had*, to handle on her own. It kept him silent, albeit observant.

"You've had a cold trip on the bayou. I'll make cocoa, no? Or coffee, if you prefer," offered Natalie. She didn't smile or acknowledge Cooper. Like him, she had eyes only for her daughter.

"I prefer to talk, *maman*." Patch felt her bones going soft. Casually she moved to the sofa arm and sat there and, to occupy her hands, removed her jacket, her gloves. Her dark brooding eyes held a fury when she raised them once again to her mother, weighing the words she knew she must speak. "It's strange to realize that Rosalina has been dead for a year and I haven't known."

Though her hands clutched the cane, Natalie seemed to crumple. "I always meant to tell you, yes."

"Why didn't you, *maman*?" Patch struggled hard to retain her dignity. It was too much to bear, with her mother's appearance, the sorrowful admission somehow making all the hopelessness real. A vein throbbed in her temple, and she opened her clenched hands and rubbed them along her pants. She knew that all eyes were on her, but she didn't care. With reluctant sympathy she watched Natalie move laboriously to the overstuffed chair and drop heavily into it, her head thrown back so that her long aristocratic neck was pulled taut. Natalie's lips worked, but it was some seconds before words emerged.

"Because at first I couldn't believe she was dead. It was like a nightmare. I expected to wake up— no?—and find Pierre alive, Rosalina well." She stared, eyes glazed, into the burning embers, then said almost inaudibly, "I wanted the money you gave me."

Patch blanched. Cooper reached out a hand to steady her, but she brushed it away, her mind swirling. Her mother had spoken the truth, but she was unable to comprehend the awfulness of it. She spoke through a tightness in her throat. "Money? What money? You mean what I gave you for Rosalina—"

"The operation money, the hospital and rest-home money. Rosalina's heart just stopped...my baby...." Natalie's fingers stroked the cane as if in stroking she could bring it to life. "During the very first operation to remove burned flesh Rosalina's heart just gave up." Her eyes locked on Patch. "There was no one to care for us except you. And if you married Arlis.... You never noticed how careless he is, what a spendthrift, how lazy...I feared that he would leave Una, and that you would take him back. I knew you blamed yourself." Natalie faltered and looked away. "When you told me of your pledge.... I'm ashamed, no? But I didn't hurt anybody. Your papa was dead, Rosalina was dead, I couldn't bring them back."

Patch could hardly speak. "You hurt *me*, *maman*. You never said it was my fault, but your every gesture, your every mention of Rosalina made my guilt worse." She felt as though she were moving and talking underwater. "What about the letters?"

"I wrote them."

"Gaston suffers, too," Patch said.

"I tried to discourage him."

Patch took note of her mother's expression, saw real fear there, the fear of poverty, of being alone, of growing old. The bitter feelings she harbored began to melt, not entirely, but enough that compassion etched her words. "What did you do with all the money?"

Natalie sagged, making a gesture with her hand that defined uselessness. "I paid the hospital bill, bought the grave and headstone. The rest...lies yonder in that drawer in the highboy...."

There still must be several thousand left, Patch thought. She suddenly felt drained. "Keep it, *maman*, use it wisely. When it runs out, I'll give you more. But I have to establish my own home now—"

"You're going to leave me, too, no?" wailed Natalie, the muscles in her face working, and Patch knew that her mother was held in bondage by her fright, her deceit. It couldn't be undone, only forgiven, and the forgiving would take a while. And so would the grieving for Rosalina. She stood up, picking up her gloves and jacket.

"I won't ever be far away, *maman*."

"Where are you going now?"

"To unload the boat."

"Eat first."

"I'm not hungry."

Natalie turned to Cooper, acknowledging his existence as she had not earlier. "M'sieu Vachec, perhaps you can make her—"

He shook his head. Patch had changed before his very eyes, becoming indomitable, more determined. He'd seen it in the set of her jaw, the gleam in her somber dark eyes. "She'll do what she wishes, what her heart says," he stated, wondering if he, too, had been cast aside. Then he followed Patch into the dogtrot.

Patch worked until she felt tattered at unloading

furs, oil barrels, laundry and sundry other items that collected from no-one-knew-where out at camp. With Cooper she shoved, hauled and pushed them up the inclining pier into the dogtrot, and those that were to go there she loaded onto her pickup. She was trying to stem the flood of rage that was perking inside her.

Cooper suspected it. The only words spoken between them were short, incisive, "Catch that...give it a hard pull...use the winch...I've got it...furs next."

At last the raw pelts were loaded and tied down in the truck bed. Patch's hands dropped to her side, and she lay her head against the cold metal side of the truck. "Nothing will ever be the same again, not with papa, or Rosalina, or *maman* or *grand-mère* or you or me! Not ever, ever, ever...oh, I hate this empty feeling!" Her voice rose with each word, and she began to beat upon the truck with her fists. Cooper stood back, staring at her long seconds, then he grabbed her hands, pulling her against his chest, holding her in a strong safe grip.

"Nothing is ever the same," he crooned. "Each and every day is different. We don't see the changes because we get up at the same time, brush our teeth the same way, hold our forks in the same hand and live always in our own little sphere. Relationships change, too, they grow or fade—"

"Or die!"

"Or die."

"*Maman* tricked me." Her voice broke. "It makes my vow seem so silly, so shoddy. When I think that Rosalina has been dead all this time...."

"Your mother is weak, like my own mother was. They had reasons that are hard for us to understand. You taught me that. You can't wallow in self-pity—"

"Don't you dare say that. Don't you dare! I hurt

and you're not helping. What right do I have for happiness?"

Cooper's look sobered and he spoke in a calm voice. "Life is for the living, Patch. You have every right—we both do. You're just too close to all that's happened. But you yourself helped me see the folly of my own hate and bitterness and guilt. I've kept myself away from happiness for so long.... Don't shake your head. I know you don't want to hear this, but your mother was doing what she thought best. Selfishly, I suppose, but she got locked into a lie and couldn't find her way out. Perhaps my own mother thought she was doing the best thing, too, leaving me behind. Perhaps she thought I'd have a better life on the farm than the transient one she lived." He grew hoarse. "I love you, Patch Chauvin. That's the long and short of it."

As the wisdom of his words went slowly through her, the wind-stirred moss hanging from thick limbs. From somewhere on the bayou a Christmas carol reached their ears. The sun was a saffron glow moving westward, trailing purple shadows across the damp swamp amid forests of pine and cypress. How could she push Cooper away now? She needed him, yet a protest still rose to her lips. "I feel such an irreparable loss, it doesn't seem fair that...that Rosalina died while I live."

He pushed her away slightly so that he could tilt her face to his. "Gaston gave me a message for you. He said to tell you that he and Rosalina were married in the eyes of God, twice."

"You mean...?"

"I'm sure it's what Gaston meant."

She buried her head on his chest. "Oh, Cooper, I'm so glad. That bothered me most of all—that she died so young without ever having known that wonderful...what you and I—"

He smiled down at her. "You know, we've never been on a real date. Suppose we wash up, put on something dressy and I'll take you to dinner."

"I'm not at all hungry."

"No one eats on first dates," he replied, happy because she had not refused and because there still was a place in her life for him. Yet a sense of urgency swelled within him, telling him that he had to make the most of the moment.

16

SITTING ACROSS A TABLE FROM HER UPSTAIRS in the Chart House on Jackson Square, Cooper observed Patch with a satisfied smile. "I asked you out to dinner and here we are. The drive did you good. Admit it."

"I thought you meant Catahoula or Henderson, *not* New Orleans!" A trace of disbelief still lingered in her voice. "And to have supper in the French Quarter!"

"A first date ought to be something special, as special as you are," he added as his eyes roved over her. She was wearing a woolen shirtwaist, pleated down the front with buttons from Peter Pan collar to hem. And she looked uncharacteristically every inch a lady, the look enhanced by a light touch of makeup and a fragrant perfume. She was strikingly beautiful, fragile and sad.

Cooper longed to feel her breasts in his hands and mouth, to taste her saucy sweet nipples with his tongue and to lose himself in her silken body. She had suffered so much, was still suffering. It was in her eyes, haunted and filled with grief. He was in an unconscionably delicate situation—how to balance her grief with the love he knew she had for him. He must show her the way, share her grief somehow.... "Do you realize this is the first time I've ever seen you in a dress? And all I can think of is how to get you out of it?"

She laughed softly, becoming a shade less doleful.

"If you start talking about sex now, I'm sure I'll never be able to eat."

"How about after dinner?"

She tried to look away from him and couldn't. "I'll...I'll listen, prob'ly."

He reached for her hand and held it, the most intimacy he dared until an hour later, when he hired a hansom cab pulled by a swaybacked nag wearing a wilting Christmas wreath about its neck.

"I wish you'd quit staring at me," Patch said, feeling a spark of erotic excitement deep inside where she thought it had died forever.

"I can't help it. If you knew just how damned good you look...." He left it at that, and directed the cabbie to the Guilbeaux Hotel, where he propelled her into the Pirate's Cove and ordered them each Drambuie and soda. After the drinks came, he lit a cigarette and let out a great breath. For a moment, as they sat there facing each other across the table, neither of them spoke. Patch's smile was tentative, and in the subdued light her large dark eyes had never been brighter. Cooper shook his head. "I don't know how to do this."

"Do what?" She toyed with the stemmed glass.

His face suddenly looked bone weary. "We haven't settled things between us." He leaned back against the banquette, letting the flickering candlelight fill his eyes, then closed them.

"But—"

He opened his eyes. "Wait. Before you say anything, let me finish." *Before my courage fails me,* he thought. "We've been through quite a lot together. You've taught me the ways of the swamp, how to trap, how to love.... We've survived the worst freeze in a century, an attack by coy-dogs—" one of his renegade smiles transformed his face "—and delivered a baby." His tongue was running away with him, but he couldn't stop now. "You once told me that you had the right to love. Well, I have that right, too, and—"

Patch touched her fingertips to his lips, hushing him. "I haven't stopped loving you. I'm only worried that I went about it all wrong." Her thick lashes fluttered, revealing the sweetly brooding depths of her eyes. "I—I'm still trying to absorb everything that's happened. I understand *maman* being scared, but I feel so...betrayed."

"You're one up on me. I never understood my own mother's motives." There was no bitterness now, only a sorrowful intensity.

"You could if you think on it, no? Back then your *maman* was prob'ly very pretty and young, and the outside world looked wonderful compared to that root cellar. Perhaps she felt hemmed in, lost even."

Cooper's eyes filled with banished memories. "I was lost."

"And now?"

"And now you've found me." He stared intently into Patch's face. "I don't know if this is the right time, I know you want a wedding, one of those fancy—"

The corners of Patch's lovely mouth tilted up, the smile transforming her expression into something almost ethereal. "If I've found you, is this finders keepers, *m'sieu*?"

Heart thundering, Cooper forced himself to be calm. "My darling Patch, there's no way you could rid yourself of me, short of feeding me to an alligator." His fingers traced the shape of her mouth, moving slowly to her temple where a delicate blue vein throbbed beneath a stray curl. "I have a confession to make."

She stiffened imperceptibly. "For a little sin or a

big one?'' Perhaps there was another landlady in his background, one that wasn't quite so old.

"You decide," he said, watching her expression. "I've reserved us a suite in this hotel."

She took a sip of Drambuie to dampen her dry throat. "I didn't bring a nightgown or a toothbrush."

"We'll order up toothbrushes," he said, cursing the quavering in his voice.

"I want you more than I can ever tell you, Cooper, but I'm not sure it's the way to mourn Rosalina—"

"Then I'll let you sleep in my arms. But I don't think she would wish you not to love, Patch. I think Rosalina would want you to cling to everything that's alive, everything that's good. It may not have been mourning, but you did dedicate a year of your life to her."

"It was wasted."

"No," he murmured with infinite gentleness. "I'm remembering that first morning when your grandmother said fate was the province of God. Don't you think He gave you that year of sacrifice in lieu of mourning?"

Patch propped her chin in her hands, reflective, suddenly hesitant. "I hadn't thought of it that way, but yes." She wavered. "What will the people in the hotel think if we go upstairs together?"

Cooper paused to inhale sharply. "They'll think that we're in love."

Ten minutes later she sat, fully dressed except for her shoes, on the edge of a huge bed in an elegant suite on the eighth floor.

Cooper pushed her gently down on the bed, adjusting the pillows.

She reached for him. "Don't leave me. I want you here in bed with me."

He slid down beside her and she turned into him,

arms sliding about his neck. And suddenly, like a
dam bursting, all the pain, all the savage anguish
flowed out of her and she started to cry—slow bitter
tears for her mother's deceit, for Rosalina's unjust
death, for what might have been. Cooper soothed
her, his lips on her forehead as one might sooth a
child, and after a while she slept.

Moonlight flooded the room when she next stirred.
"Cooper?"

His arm tightened about her. "I'm awake."

"I didn't mean to go all—"

"We're going to be married, Patch. If not tomorrow, the next day. I've been thinking. In the morning we'll drive to Baton Rouge, to the cematery—"

"Yes, I'd like that." Her voice dropped very low as
she felt for the right words. "I think I could make
love now. That is, if you still want to."

She heard his indrawn breath as he took her hand
and placed it on his hard shaft. "Is that answer
enough for you?" Then he reached for her shoulders. As she raised her head, he lowered his mouth
to hers. Only in that way did they touch, his hands
on her shoulders, his lips upon hers, until she
brushed his hands aside and began to unbutton her
dress.

"I'll do that...." His big fingers trembled in the
moonlight as he tried to shove each tiny disk through
its loop, concerned that he'd rip them out in his impatience. Finally, finally, the dress and slip fell away
from her shoulders, over her breasts, baring them.
Cooper kissed each soft mound, drew at each nipple,
until they had risen as firmly as his own flesh.

"Tell me you love me, Cooper."

"I love you...love you...."

Her hands went to his shirt, his belt, and in a moment he was more naked than she. "There will
never be anyone else...?"

"Never, only you," and he removed the clothes
that remained between them. For a moment he
looked down on her, looked down on her flushed
comeliness, looked down on that treasure of sweet
cream flesh.... "I'm starved for want of you. It
seems like a thousand years since we've made love."

"*Maman* and *grand-mère* are going to be worried—"

"No, I told your grandmother not to expect us
back tonight." He took her into his arms and began
to stroke her smooth soft skin. With a little cry she
moved to offer herself, hot, naked, loving.

Cooper moaned gutturally, burying his lips in the
very small valley between her breasts, floating over
the softness of her belly, her coltish thighs. His
tongue touched her open wanting flesh, thrusting
into sweet moist hollows, and time lost meaning as
she gave herself over to the grand and sensuous pas-
sions that engulfed her.

Then for a time the night seemed to stand still.
When Cooper would have thrust himself between
her thighs, she gave a tiny push with her knee, stopping him. Her mouth found him hungrily, bruis-
ingly. She talked to him in Cajun French, loving
him, naming every body part that her lips touched,
making up stories about this man-part or that, with
Cooper wondering what in hell she was saying until
her lips finished one story, one place, and went on to
another. Then he didn't care what the words were,
for the language her hands and mouth spoke was
eminently decipherable, and he was consumed in
that final fire.

Later, as she lay in his arms while her hands still
crept over him here and there, just to see if certain
parts remained active, they talked. "Why does your
beard grow so dark when the rest of you is so
blond?" she asked drowsily.

"Ask me something else," Cooper declared, his mind more on where her hands traveled than on sorting out nature's mysteries.

Patch thought a minute. "Do you think God creates each soul, or that parents make the soul when they make the baby?"

Cooper dragged his free hand over his face, expelling a cryptic moan. "Do you know that you're the only woman I know who always manages to talk about God in bed? Couldn't we just talk about sex?"

Patch raised up and glared at him in the dark. "Perhaps we should talk about those other women, no?"

"God will do," he said dryly, tightening his arm, forcing her down on the bed next to him so that he could nibble on her ear. "Now talk," he ordered in a soft breath.

Her voice was silent, offering up a thank-you that God had answered her prayers and sent her a man—flawed, to be sure, but one well worth loving. She gave a fleeting thought to *grand-mère*'s trunk, to the first Angelicque to whom it had belonged and who had made a good marriage. And so would she, Patch thought. She turned her head so that her lips brushed Cooper's, feeling the need in him swelling against her own silken thighs and his hands cupping her small upthrusting breasts.

Perhaps not so flawed, she thought, and took him into her.

HARLEQUIN
PREMIERE AUTHOR EDITIONS

6 EXCITING HARLEQUIN AUTHORS — 6 OF THEIR BEST BOOKS!

Daphne Clair
A STREAK OF GOLD

Marjorie Lewty
TO CATCH A BUTTERFLY

Anne Mather
SCORPIONS' DANCE

Jessica Steele
SPRING GIRL

Margaret Way
THE WILD SWAN

Violet Winspear
DESIRE HAS NO MERCY

EYE OF THE STORM

MAURA SEGER

A powerful portrayal of the events of World War II in the Pacific, *Eye of the Storm* is a riveting story of how love triumphs over hatred. In this, the first of a three book chronicle, Army nurse Maggie Lawrence meets Marine Sgt. Anthony Gargano. Despite military regulations against fraternization, they resolve to face together whatever lies ahead.... Also known by her fans as Laurel Winslow, Sara Jennings, Anne MacNeil and Jenny Bates, Maura Seger, author of this searing novel, was named by ROMANTIC TIMES as 1984's Most Versatile Romance Author.

At your favorite bookstore in March.

EYE-B-1